PENGUIN BOOKS

WORLD'S END

Paul Theroux was born in Medford, Massachusetts, in 1941, and published his first novel, *Waldo*, in 1967. He wrote his next three novels, *Fang and the Indians*, *Girls at Play* and *Jungle Lovers*, after a five-year stay in Africa. He subsequently taught at the University of Singapore, and during his three years there produced a collection of short stories, *Sinning with Annie*, and his highly praised novel, *Saint Jack*. His other publications include *The Black House* (1974), *The Great Railway Bazaar* (1975), *The Family Arsenal* (1976), *The Consul's File* (1977), *Picture Palace* (1978; winner of the Whitbread Literary Award), *A Christmas Card* (1978), a short story illustrated by John Lawrence, *The Old Patagonian Express* (1979), *London Snow* (1980), *The Mosquito Coast* (1981), which was the *Yorkshire Post* Novel of the Year for 1981 and the joint winner of the James Tait Black Memorial Prize, *The London Embassy* (1982), and *The Kingdom by the Sea* (1983).

Paul Theroux lives in London with his wife and two children.

PAUL THEROUX

WORLD'S END
AND OTHER STORIES

PENGUIN BOOKS

Penguin Books Ltd, Harmondsworth, Middlesex, England
Viking Penguin Inc., 40 West 23rd Street, New York, New York 10010, U.S.A.
Penguin Books Australia Ltd, Ringwood, Victoria, Australia
Penguin Books Canada Ltd, 2801 John Street, Markham, Ontario, Canada L3R 1B4
Penguin Books (N.Z.) Ltd, 182–190 Wairau Road, Auckland 10, New Zealand

First published by Hamish Hamilton Ltd 1980
Published in Penguin Books 1982
Reprinted 1982, 1984

Made and printed in Great Britain by
Hazell Watson & Viney Limited,
Member of the BPCC Group,
Aylesbury, Bucks
Set in Baskerville

Some of the stories in this collection first appeared in the following publications: 'World's End' in *Mademoiselle*; 'Zombies', 'Algebra', and 'The English Adventure' in *Punch*; 'The Imperial Icehouse' in the *Atlantic* and the *New Statesman*; 'Yard Sale' and 'Acknowledgments' in the *New Yorker*; 'After the War' in *Redbook* and *Punch*; 'Words Are Deeds' in *Harper's Magazine* and the *Tatler*; 'White Lies' in *Playboy*; 'Clapham Junction' in the *New Statesman*; 'The Odd-Job Man' in the *Atlantic* and *The Times* (London); 'The Greenest Island' in the *New Review*.

FOR
JOYCE HARTMAN

CONTENTS

WORLD'S END

ROBARGE WAS a happy man who had taken a great risk. He had transplanted his family — his wife and small boy — from their home in America to a bizarrely named but buried-alive district called World's End in London, where they were strangers. It had worked, and it made his happiness greater. His wife, Kathy, had changed. Having overcome this wrench from home and mastered the new routine, she became confident. It showed in her physically — she had unstiffened; she adopted a new hairstyle; she slimmed; she had been set free by proving to her husband that he depended on her. Richard, only six, was already in what Robarge regarded as the second grade: the little boy could read and write! Even Robarge's company, a supplier of drilling equipment for offshore oil rigs, was pleased by the way he had managed; they associated their success with Robarge's hard work.

So Robarge was vindicated in the move he had made. He had considered marriage the quietest enactment of sharing, connubial exclusiveness the most private way to live — a sheltered life in the best sense. And he saw England as upholding the domestic reverences that had been tossed aside in America. He had not merely moved his family but rescued them. His sense of security made him feel younger, an added pleasure.

He did not worry about growing old; he had put on weight in these four years at World's End and began to affect that curious sideways gait, almost a limp, of a heavy boy. It was a game — he was nearly forty — but games were still possible in this country where he could go unrecognized and so unmocked.

Most of all, he liked returning home in the rain. The house at World's End was a refuge; he could shut his door on the darkness and smell the straightness of his own rooms. The yellow lights from the street showed the rain droplets patterned on the window, and he could hear it falling outside, the drip from the sky, as irregular as a weeping tree, which meant in London that it would go on all night. Tonight he was returning from Holland — a Dutch subsidiary machined the drilling bits he dispatched to Aberdeen.

Without waking Kathy, he took the slender parcel he had carried from Amsterdam and crept upstairs to his son's room. On the plane he had kept it on his lap — there was nowhere to stow it. A man in the adjoining seat had stared and prompted Robarge to say, "It's a kite. For my son. The Dutch import them from the Far East. Supposed to be foolproof." The man had answered him by taking out a pair of binoculars he had bought for his own boy at the duty-free shop.

"Richard's only six," said Robarge.

The man said that the older children got the more expensive they were. He said it affectionately and with pride, and Robarge thought how glad he would be when Richard was old enough to appreciate a really expensive present — skis, a camera, a pocket calculator, a radio. Then he would know how his father loved him and how there was nothing in the world he would not give him. And he felt a casual envy for the man in the next seat, having a son old enough to want the things his father could afford. His own uncomprehending son asked for nothing: it made fiercer Robarge's desire to show his love.

The lights in the house were out; it was, at midnight, as gloomy as a tunnel and seemed narrow and empty in all that darkness. Richard's door was ajar. Robarge went in and found his son sleeping peacefully under wall posters of dinosaurs and fighter planes. Robarge knelt and kissed the boy, then sat on the bed and delighted in hearing the boy's measured breaths. The breaths stopped. In the harsh knife of light falling through the curtains from the street Robarge saw his son stir.

"Hello." The word came whole: Richard's voice was wide-awake.

"It's me." He kissed the boy. "Look what I brought you."

Robarge brandished the parcel. There was a film of rain on the plastic wrapper.

"What is it?" Richard asked.

Robarge told him: A kite. "Now go back to sleep like a good boy."

"Can we fly it?"

"You bet. If it's windy we'll fly it at the park."

"It's not windy enough at the park. You have to go in the car."

"Where shall we go?"

"Box Hill's a good place for kites."

"Is it windy there?"

"Not half!" whispered the child.

Robarge was delighted by this odd English expression in his son's speech, and he muttered it to himself in amazement. He was gladdened by Richard's response; he had pondered so long at the gift shop at Schiphol wondering which toy to buy — like an eager indecisive child himself — he had nearly missed his flight.

"Box Hill it is then." It meant a long drive, but the next day was Saturday — he could devote his weekend to the boy. He crossed the hall and undressed in the dark. When he got into the double bed, Kathy touched his arm and murmured, "You're back," and she swung over and sighed and pulled the blankets closer.

*   *   *

"I think I made a hit last night," said Robarge over breakfast. He told Kathy about the kite.

"You mean you woke him up to give him that thing?"

Kathy's tone discouraged him: he had hoped she would be glad. He said, "He was already awake — I heard him calling out. Must have had a bad dream. I went straight up." All these lies to conceal his impulsive wish to kiss his sleeping child at midnight. "We'll fly the thing today if there's any wind."

"That's nice," said Kathy. Her voice was flat and unfocused, almost belittling.

"Anything wrong?"

She said no and got up from the table, which was her abrupt way of showing boredom or changing the subject. And yet Robarge was struck by how attractive she was; how, without noticeable effort, she had discovered the kind of glamour a younger woman might envy. She was thin and had soft heavy breasts and wore light expensive blouses with her jeans.

Robarge said, "Are you angry because I travel so much?"

"You take your job seriously," she said. "Don't apologize. I haven't nagged you about that."

"I'm lucky I'm based in London — think of the rest of them in Aberdeen. How would you like to be there?"

"Don't say it in that threatening way. I wouldn't go to Aberdeen."

"I might have been posted there." He said it loudly, with the confidence of one who has been reprieved.

"You would have gone alone." He guessed she was poking fun; he was grateful for that, grateful that things had worked out so well in London.

"You didn't want to come here," he said. "But you're glad now, aren't you?"

Kathy did not reply. She was clearing the table and at the same time setting out Richard's breakfast.

"Aren't you?" he repeated in a taunting way.

"Yes!" she said, with unreasonable force, reddening as she spoke. Then she burst into tears. "There," she stuttered, "are you satisfied?"

Robarge, made guilty by her outburst (what had he said?), approached his wife to calm her. But she turned away. He heard Richard on the stairs, and the rattle of the kite dragging. He saw with relief that Kathy had fled into the kitchen, where Richard could not hear her sobbing.

*   *   *

He had dropped Kathy on the Kings Road and proceeded — Richard in the back seat — out of London toward Box Hill. It was only then that he remembered that he had failed to tell Kathy where they were going. She hadn't asked: her tears had made her stubbornly silent. It was late May and once they were past Epsom he could see bluebells growing thickly in the shade of pine woods, and the pale green of the new leaves of beeches, and — already high and drooping from the weight of their blossoms — the cow parsley at the margins of plowed fields.

Richard said, "There are seagulls here."

Robarge smiled. There were no seagulls — only newly plowed fields set off by windbreaks of pines, and some crows fussing from tree to tree, to squawk.

"The black ones are crows."

"But seagulls are white," said Richard. "They follow the tractor and eat the worms when the farmer digs them up."

"You're a smart boy. But seagulls — "

"There they are," said Richard.

The child was right; at the edge of a field a tractor turned and just behind it, hovering and swooping — seagulls.

They parked near the Burford Bridge Hotel, and above

them Robarge saw the long scar of exposed chalk, a whole eroded chute of it, and the steep green hill rising beside it to the brow of a grassy slope where the woods began.

"Mind the cars," said Richard, warning his father. They paused at the road near the parking lot. A motorcyclist sped past, then the child led his father across. He was being tugged by the child to the far left of a clump of boulders at the base of the hill, and then he saw the nearly hidden path. He realized he was being led by the boy to this entrance, then up the path beside the chalk slide to the gentler rise of the hill. Here Richard broke away and ran the rest of the way up the slope.

"Shall we fly it here?"

"No — over there," said Richard, out of breath and pointing at nothing Robarge could see. "Where it's windy."

They resumed, Robarge trudging, the child leading, until they were on the ridge of the hill. It was as the child had said, for no sooner had he walked to the highest point on that part of the hill than Robarge felt the wind. The path was sheltered, but here the wind was so strong it almost tore the kite from his hands. Robarge was proud of his son for leading him here.

"This is fun!" said Richard excitedly, as Robarge fixed the crosspiece and looped the twine, tightening and flattening the paper butterfly. He took the ball of string from his pocket and fastened it to the kite.

Richard said, "What about the tail?"

"This kite doesn't need a tail. It's foolproof."

"All kites need tails," Richard said. "Or they fall down."

The certainty in the child's voice irritated Robarge. He said, "Don't be silly," and raised the kite and let the wind pull it from his hand. The kite rose, spun, and then plummeted to the ground. Robarge tried this two more times and then, fearing that he would destroy the frail thing, he squatted and saw that a bit of it was torn.

"It's broken!" Richard shrieked.

"That won't make any difference."

"It needs a tail!" the child cried.

Robarge was annoyed by the child's insistence. It was the monotonous pedantry he had used in speaking about the seagulls. Robarge said, "We haven't got a tail."

Richard planted his feet apart and peered at the kite with his large serious face and said, "Your necktie can be a tail."

"I don't know whether you've noticed, Rich, but I'm not wearing a necktie."

"It won't work then," said the child. Robarge thought for a moment that the child was going to stamp on the kite in rage. He kicked the ground and said tearfully, "I told you it needs a tail!"

"Maybe we can use something else. How about a handkerchief?"

"No — just a tie. Or it won't work."

Robarge pulled out his handkerchief and tore it into three strips. These he knotted together to make a streamer for the tail. He tied it to the bottom corner of the kite, and while Richard sulked on the grass, Robarge, by running in circles, got the kite aloft. He tugged it and paid out string and made it bob; soon the kite was steadied on the curvature of white line. Richard was beside him, happy again, hopping on his small bow legs.

Robarge said, "You were right about the tail."

"Can I have a go?"

A go! Robarge had begun to smile again. "You want a go, huh? Think you can do it?"

"I know how," said Richard.

Robarge handed his son the string and watched him lean back and draw the kite higher. Robarge encouraged him. Instead of smiling, the child was made serious by the praise. He worked the string back and forth and said nothing.

"That's it," said Robarge. "You're an expert."

Richard held the string over his head. He made the kite

climb and dance. The wind beat against the paper. The child said, "I told you it needed a tail."

"You're doing very well. Walk backward and you'll tighten the line."

But Richard, to Robarge's approval, wound the string on the ball. The kite began to rise. Robarge was impatient to fly the kite himself. He said he could get it much higher and then demanded his turn. He got the kite very high and while it swung he said, "You're a smart boy. I wouldn't have thought of coming here. And you're good at this. Next time I'll get you a bigger kite — not a paper one, but plastic. They can go hundreds of feet up."

"That's against the law."

"Don't be silly."

"Yes. You can get arrested. It makes the planes crash," said the child. "In England."

Robarge was still making sweeping motions with the string, lifting the kite, making it dive. "Who says?"

"A man told me."

Robarge snorted. "What man?"

"Mummy's friend."

The child screamed. The kite was falling on its broken string. It crashed against the hill and came apart, blowing until it was misshapen. Robarge thought: I am blind.

* * *

Later, when the child was calm and the broken kite stuffed beneath a bush (Robarge promised to buy a new one), he confirmed what Robarge had feared: he had been there before, seen the gulls, climbed the hill, and the man — he had no name, he was "Mummy's friend" — had taken off his necktie to make a tail for the kite.

The man had worn a tie. Robarge created a lover from this detail and saw someone middle aged, middle class, perhaps prosperous, a serious rival, out to impress — British, of course.

He saw the man's hand slipped beneath one of Kathy's brilliant silk blouses. He wondered whether he knew the man; but who did they know? They had been happy and solitary in this foreign country, at World's End. He wanted to cry. He felt his face breaking to expose all his sadness.

"Want to see my hide-out?"

The child showed Robarge the fallen tree, the pine grove, the stumps.

"Did Mummy's friend play with you?"

"The first time — "

Kathy had gone there twice with her lover and Richard! Robarge wanted to leave the place, but the child ran from tree to tree, remembering the games they had played.

Robarge said, "Were they nice picnics?"

"Not half!"

It was the man's expression, he was sure; and now he hated it.

"What are you looking at, Daddy?"

He was staring at the trampled pine needles, the seclusion of the trees, the narrow path.

"Nothing."

Richard did not want to go home, but Robarge insisted, and walking back to the car Robarge could not prevent himself from asking questions to which he did not want to hear answers.

The man's name?

"I don't know."

Did he have a nice car?

"Blue." The child looked away.

"What did Mummy's friend say to you?"

"I don't remember." Now Richard ran ahead, down the hill.

He saw that the child was disturbed. If he pressed too hard he would frighten him. And so they drove back to World's End in silence.

* * *

Robarge did not tell Kathy where they had gone, and instead of confronting her with what he knew he watched her. He did not want to lose her in an argument; it was easy to imagine the terrible scene — her protests, her lies. She might not deny it, he thought; she might make it worse.

He directed his anger against the man. He wanted to kill him, to save himself. That night he made love to Kathy in a fierce testing way, as if challenging her to refuse. But she submitted to his bullying and at last, as he lay panting beside her, she said, "Are you finished?"

*   *   *

A few days later, desperate to know whether his wife's love had been stolen from him, Robarge told Kathy that he had to go to Aberdeen on business.

"When will you be back?"

"I'm not sure." He thought: Why should I make it easier on her? "I'll call you."

But she accepted this as she had accepted his wordless assault on her, and it seemed to him as though nothing had happened, she had no lover, she had been loyal. He had only the child's word. But the child was innocent and had never lied.

On the morning of his departure for Aberdeen he went to Richard's room. He shut the door and said, "Do you love me?"

The child moved his head and stared.

"If you really love me, you won't tell Mummy what I'm going to ask you to do."

"I won't tell."

"When I'm gone, I want you to be the daddy."

Richard's face grew solemn.

"That means you have to be very careful. You have to make sure that Mummy's all right."

"Why won't Mummy be all right?"

Robarge said, "I think her friend is a thief."

"No — he's not!"

"Don't be upset," said Robarge. "That's what we're going to find out. I want you to watch him if he comes over again."

"But why? Don't you like him?"

"I don't know him very well — not as well as Mummy does. Will you watch him for me, like a daddy?"

"Yes."

"If you do, I'll bring you a nice present."

"Mummy's friend gave me a present."

Robarge was so startled he could not speak; and he wanted to shout. The child peered at him, and Robarge saw curiosity and pity mingled in the child's squint.

"It was a little car."

"I'll give you a big car," Robarge managed.

"What's he stealing from you, Daddy?"

Robarge thought a moment, then said, "Something very precious — " and his voice broke. If he forced it he would sob. He left the child's room. He had never felt sadder.

Downstairs, Kathy kissed him on his ear. The smack of it caused a ringing in a horn in his head.

*   *   *

He had invented the trip to Aberdeen; he invented work to justify it, and for three days he knew what madness was — a sickening and a sorrow. He was deaf, his feet and hands were stupid, and his tongue at times seemed to swell and choke him when he tried to speak. He wanted to tell his area supervisor that he was suffering, that he knew how odd he must appear. But he did not know how to begin. And strangely, though his behavior was clumsily childlike, he felt elderly, as if he were dying inside, all his organs working feebly. He returned to London feeling that a burned hole was blackened on his heart.

The house at World's End was so still that in the doorway he considered that she was gone, that she had taken Richard and deserted him with her lover. This was Sunday evening, part of his plan — a surprise: he usually returned on Monday.

He was not reassured to see the kitchen light on — there was a telephone in the kitchen. But Kathy's face, when she answered the door, was blank.

She said, "I thought you might call from the station."

He tried to kiss her — she pulled away.

"My hands are wet."

"Glad to see me?"

"I'm doing the dishes." She lost her look of boredom and said, "You're so pale."

"I haven't slept." He could not gather the phrases of the question in his mind because he dreaded the simple answer he saw whole: yes. He felt afraid of her, and more deaf and clumsy than ever, like a helpless orphan snatched into the dark. He wanted her to say that he had imagined the lover, but he knew he would not believe words he craved so much to hear. He no longer trusted her and would not trust her until he had the child's word. He longed to see his son. He started up the stairs.

Kathy said, "He's watching television."

On entering the television room, Robarge saw his son stand up and take a step backward. Richard's face in the darkened room was the yellow-green hue of the television screen; his hands sprang to his ears; the blue fibers of his pajamas glowed as if sprinkled with salt. When Robarge switched on the light the child ran to him and held him — so tightly that Robarge could not hug him.

"Here it is." Robarge disengaged himself from the child and crossed the room, turning off the television as he went. The toy was gift wrapped in bright paper and tied with a ribbon. He handed it to Richard. Richard put his face against his father's neck. "Aren't you going to open it?"

Robarge felt the child nodding against his shoulder.

"Time for bed," said Robarge.

The child said, "I put myself to bed now."

"All by yourself?" said Robarge. "Okay, off you go then."

Richard went to the door.

"Don't forget your present!"

Richard hesitated. Robarge brought it to him and tucked it under the child's arm. Then, pretending it was an afterthought, he said softly, "Tell me what happened while I was away — did you see anything?"

Richard shook his head and let his mouth gape.

"What about Mummy's friend?" Robarge was standing; the question dropped to the child like a spider lowering on its own filament of spittle.

"I didn't see him."

The child looked so small; Robarge towered over him. He knelt and asked, "Are you telling the truth?"

And it occurred to Robarge that he had never asked the child that question before — had never used that intimidating tone or looked so hard into the child's eyes. Richard backed away, the gift-wrapped parcel under his arm.

At this little distance, the child seemed calmer. He shook his head as he had before, but this time his confidence was pronounced, as if in the minute that had elapsed he had learned the trick of it. With the faintest trace of a stutter — when had he ever stuttered? — he said, "It's the truth, Daddy. I didn't."

Robarge said, "It's a tank. The batteries are already inside. It shoots sparks." Then he shuffled forward on his knees and took the child's arm. "You'll tell me if you see that man again, won't you?"

Richard stared.

"I mean, if he steals anything?"

Robarge saw corruption in the unblinking eyes.

"You'll tell me, won't you?"

When Robarge repeated the question, Richard said, "Mummy doesn't have a friend," and Robarge knew he had lost the child.

He said, "Show me how you put yourself to bed."

Robarge was unconsoled. He found Kathy had already

gone to bed, and though the light was on she lay on her side, facing the dark wall, as if sleeping.

Robarge said, "We never make love."

"We did — on Wednesday."

She was right; he had forgotten.

She said, "I've locked the doors. Will you make sure the lights are out?"

So he went from room to room turning out the lights, and in the television room Robarge sat down in the darkness. There, in the house which now seemed to be made of iron, he remembered again that he was in London, in World's End; that he had taken his family there. He was saddened by the thought that he was so far from home. The darkness hid him and hid the country; he knew that if he appeared calm it was only because the darkness concealed his loss. He wished he had never come here, and worrying this way he craved his child and had a hideous reverie, of wishing to eat the child and eat his wife and keep them in that cannibal way. Burdened by this guilty thought, he went upstairs to make sure his son was safe.

Richard was in darkness, too. Robarge kissed the child's hot cheek. There was a bright cube on the floor, the present from Aberdeen. He picked it up and saw that it had not been opened.

He put it beside Richard on the bed and leaning for balance he pressed something in the bedclothes. It was long and flat and the hardness stung his hand. It was the breadknife with the serrated blade from the kitchen, tucked beneath these sheets, close to the child's body. Breathless from the shock of it Robarge took it away.

And then he went to bed. He was shaking so badly he did not think he would ever sleep. He wanted to smash his face against the wall and hit it until it was bloody and he had torn his nose away. He dropped violently to sleep. When he woke in the dark he recalled the sound that had wakened him — it was still vibrant in the air, the click of the front gate: a thief was entering his house. Robarge waited for more, and perspired. His fear left him and he was penetrated by the fake vitality of insomnia. After an hour he decided that what he had heard, if anything, was a thief leaving the house, not breaking in. Too late, too far, too dark, he thought; and he knew now they were all lost.

ZOMBIES

MISS BRISTOW was certain she had dreamed of a skull because on waking — gasping to the parlor and throwing open the curtains — the first face she had seen was skull-like, a man or woman looking directly in at her from the 49 bus. It verified her dream but was simpler and so more horrible, with staring eyes and bony cheeks and sharp teeth and the long strings of dirty hair they called dreadlocks. She went to the small cabinet and plucked at the doors with clumsy fingers before she remembered that Alison had the key. And then she felt abandoned in dismal terror, between the bedroom where she had dreamed the skull and the window where she had seen the face moving down Sloane Street.

She was still in her slippers and robe when Alison arrived at ten. Alison was an efficient girl with powerful shoulders, a nurse's sliding tread and humor in her whole body; the distress was confined to her eyes. She said, "Have we had a good night?"

Miss Bristow did not reply to the question. She was tremulous with thought. Her arthritis gave her the look of someone cowering.

"You took the key."

Alison appeared not to hear her. "I hope you haven't forgotten that you have a lunch date today."

She had forgotten. She saw the skull, the teeth, the cowl of hair grinning from the far side of a table in a restaurant where she was trapped. She said, "Who is it?"

"Philippa — that nice girl from Howletts. She left a message last week."

Miss Bristow was relieved. She said, "The Italian."

"Philippa is not Italian," said Alison in the singsong she used when she repeated herself. "Now you must put some clothes on. You haven't had your bath." She opened the blue diary and said, "She's coming here at twelve. She'll have news of your book."

"In a moment you're going to say you've lost the key."

Alison said, "We promised we weren't going to be naughty, didn't we?"

* * *

The Italian, she thought in her bath. At the party, months ago, the girl Philippa had sat at her feet and a sentence was fully framed in Miss Bristow's mind. "I can remember," she said, rapping the words on the arm of her chair, struggling to say them, "I can remember when we were Romans."

"And now we're Italians," the girl had said quickly.

Miss Bristow peered at the girl's blank face. The girl scarcely knew how witty she had been, and so Miss Bristow felt better about appropriating the remark and making it her own: *We are Romans turning into Italians*.

The girl had been attentive, with a hearty dedication, saying, "Your glass is empty again!" But the criticism in the words was not in her tone. Miss Bristow felt the need to sip; she panicked and became breathless when there was nothing to sip. But the girl had made sure there was something in the glass all evening. Miss Bristow sensed the girl's watchfulness as she sipped. How could she explain the paradox she herself did not understand? The contents of this glass worsened her fears, but made her better able to bear them.

"I take no pleasure in this," said Miss Bristow. "It is a necessity, like a splint on a fracture."

Or, she thought, *embalming fluid*. At eighty-two, Miss Bristow felt like a corpse. A celebrated writer in the thirties, she had, after a period of obscurity, lived on to see her work rediscovered and treated — those angry and unhappy books — with a serene reverence. The critical essays about her had the slightly fraudulent forgiving tone of obituaries, publication days the solemnity of exhumations. She knew the talk, that people believed she had been dead for years. When it was learned (and this was news in London) that she was not dead, but had only fallen silent, living on gin in solitude in a tiny Welsh village, she was invited to parties. The books that were republished sold well. She was regarded as a survivor, a voice from the past. And part of her past, the earliest, was a small island in the Caribbean. For the first time in her life, she could afford to live in London. She could not remember when people had listened to her so keenly. She began to write again.

Philippa had asked all the predictable questions, and then they had started to discuss the country. Strangers meeting in London these days spoke of the condition of England as they had once spoken of the weather — cherishing the subject, as people did a harmless illness or a plucky defeat. England was in a pickle: they made it comedy, without consequences, as the girl had done: "And now we're Italians."

All evening Miss Bristow had been in the chair. Philippa had carried drinks to her, and a heaped plate of food from the buffet downstairs. Miss Bristow had eaten a pinch of watercress and some of the swollen raisins from the risotto. The ease made her reflective, and the girl relaxed, too.

"I love it here," said Philippa. "So many literary people!"

"Do you think so?" Miss Bristow liked the girl's dullness. Lively people required listeners and close attention.

"Sarah's fantastic."

"That woman," said Miss Bristow, indicating Sarah, the

hostess, who was a poet's widow. "She is to her late husband's work what Anne Hathaway's cottage is to *Hamlet*."

Philippa moved her lips and laughed.

Miss Bristow said, "And I am a zombie."

Miss Bristow was aware that her fame made bright people shy. But the girl was dull and bold. She was attentive without fawning. She was carelessly pretty, like a beauty in an old snapshot. Miss Bristow wanted to know the girl better, not so much to make a friend as to reacquaint herself with the person she had once been. Already she had seen the reenactment of some of her own traits — going downstairs for the food the girl had flirted with a black man; she had a slyness in her stare; she knelt on the floor unselfconsciously; she had a frank laugh and a nervous cough — the sounds were harshly similar and seemed to give no relief.

Miss Bristow had been like this — hard and pretty and reckless in ways that had later, as memories, lessened her loneliness. She had emerged from her twenty years' solitude whole, impatient, her imagination undiminished and with an added strength, a directness. She hated discussion, talk of terms, Howletts' ritual respect whenever she turned in a new book. And memory: years of her life which she had thought irretrievable, when she had been as young as that girl, she recovered and wrote about. It startled her to remember these years — other lives in another world. She was glad that she had that girl to talk to. She was, she felt, speaking to her younger self.

"I hope it's not too strong," said Philippa returning again, the glass between two fingers. Miss Bristow noticed the physical difference in their hands. Her own, twisted with arthritis, was so shaped by habit that it snugly fitted the glass.

"You are so right," said Miss Bristow. "Romans turning into Italians."

Philippa looked baffled. Miss Bristow remembered: the girl had not said precisely that.

"Oh, yes," Philippa finally said. "But no one has described it better than you."

Had she? Perhaps — in a book or story long ago which had not enjoyed the revival. There had been so many books, too great a number for any disinterment to be complete. And now, like everyone else, she knew only the work that had been revived, that was spoken about. The rest was lost to her.

The girl said, "I admire your work enormously."

It was not exactly what Miss Bristow wished to hear. She felt sisterly, but her affection was being returned to her more formally, as to a grandmother or great-aunt, and it obliged her with the impulse to do something for this girl — to help her in some way, if only to prevent her from squandering her attention on worthless people like Sarah.

"Do you write?" said Miss Bristow, dreading the girl's reply.

"I tried," said Philippa. "I spent a summer in the Caribbean. I wrote poems, part of a play. I started a novel. Then I came home and burned the lot."

"Ah," sighed Miss Bristow, seeing the flames — swift and yellow, they consumed the luxury of error and wasted time. It matched a memory of hers and was too much for her. She said, "And did you visit Isabella?"

Isabella had been Miss Bristow's island.

"Only for a holiday."

"A holiday?" It dignified the place absurdly. A holiday *there!*

The girl coughed her nervous cough. She said, "More of a pilgrimage, actually. But I had been there so often already in your books it was as if I were simply returning. It is such a lovely island."

"It was lovely once." Miss Bristow thought a moment, and sipped, and said, "In Roman times."

"Changeless, like so many of those islands."

Miss Bristow said, "The Romans became Italians. It has altered beyond recognition."

"You reckon?" said Philippa.

Miss Bristow smiled at the expression.

"You really ought to go back."

"I did. I couldn't bear it. Everything has changed. I was lost — I went to the beach, for a stroll, for my sanity. It was ghastly."

"The hotels," said Philippa.

"I like hotels," said Miss Bristow. "We built our share of hotels. No, it was the tidewrack, the detritus on the sand. Once, it was all driftwood and torn nets, barrel staves, rope — beautiful things. You expected to find pirate treasure, messages in bottles. Now it is all plastic beakers, tins and tubs, broken glass, bits of rubber. Junk. And oil. And worse."

"Pollution," said Philippa.

Miss Bristow glanced at the girl, wondering if with this idiot word she was satirizing her.

"I must write about it."

"You will."

"Yes, encourage me," said Miss Bristow. She looked at her crooked fingers and she whispered, "I write so slowly now."

"No one writes about the really important things."

"Exactly," said Miss Bristow. "And what are you writing, my dear?"

Philippa said, "I think it is ever so important to realize that if one has no talent one ought not to waste one's time in self-deception. I would rather help others, who really have a gift."

"You are so right."

Philippa winced. "I am on the dole."

Miss Bristow could not hide her shock. This pretty girl, this drawing room, the talk of her holiday. For a moment, Miss Bristow thought this girl was speaking figuratively: rich parents, idleness.

"I've as much right to it as anyone else," said the girl, and as she spoke of having lost her job selling antiques, of the Employment Exchange, Miss Bristow looked at the girl's hands

— the ring, the silver bracelet: the girl collected her money with these perfect hands.

"Terrible," said Miss Bristow. "An American asked me just the other day, 'How can you live here?' I said, 'I can live here because I once lived on an island that was overrun by savages.'"

"Actually," said Philippa, "I'd like to be in publishing. But there aren't any jobs going just at the moment."

"They are the enemy," said Miss Bristow. "But if you are absolutely determined I might be able to help you. My publisher is looking for someone. Do you know Howletts?"

"They're awfully grand."

Miss Bristow laughed. "I used to think that!"

"But their list is — "

"It is all trade," said Miss Bristow. "They are in business to make money, like everyone else. In Isabella, before the Great War, there were icehouses in the capital. Yes, water was a commodity! They sold it by the cake to planters who carried it upcountry, so they could have cool drinks. The ice merchants were on to a good thing — isn't that the phrase? They might have been selling anything — cloth by the yard, soap, matches, motor cars." Miss Bristow pursed her lips and added, "Or books."

"You're being a bit unfair."

"Am I? I mean it as praise. What a very great pity it would be if they were not interested in profit," said Miss Bristow. "But they are, which is why I have no friends there."

"Drink," said Philippa briskly. And before Miss Bristow could react, her empty glass was lifted from her hand.

"You are very kind," said Miss Bristow.

The girl was immediately hired at Howletts on Miss Bristow's recommendation. And Miss Bristow knew she had assigned the girl to the firm to approve her new book, to eliminate the ritual. Miss Bristow wanted an ally. Dull people mattered more than the spirited ones who mystified her with praise that sounded like mockery.

And now, rising carefully from the bath so she would not break her bones, and hating the feeble image that made the full-length glass seem a ridiculous distorting mirror, she thought how, in the months Philippa had been at Howletts, she had been able to work. She had her ally; and she wasn't fooled: the girl knew very little of her, but how could she? The girl was as she had once been — bold and untruthful, undemanding, generous, and a little foolish. But the girl believed, and the girl did not judge her — that was worth anything. Miss Bristow remembered that she had liked the girl for a phrase, a single observation — Romans, Italians. She had put this into a story and afterward had felt grateful and a bit guilty using words that were not wholly hers. The indebtedness was nothing compared to the fears she remembered and the faces she saw, sleeping, waking, so often now as she tunneled in the past, living in it more intensely now and blinking the zombies away to write about it.

The door chimes rang. Miss Bristow became eager.

* * *

"Won't you have something to drink?" said Miss Bristow, entering the parlor, taking the girl's hand. She kept her back to the window so as not to see any skulls. This fear made her seem prim, and even somewhat stately.

Alison said, "I have already asked her. She doesn't want anything."

"Go on, my dear. A gin and tonic perhaps?"

"Oh, all right," said Philippa.

"You see?" said Miss Bristow.

Alison reached through the neck of her jumper and brought out a blunt key on a thong. She went to the cabinet, removed the gin bottle, and made Philippa's drink.

"I will join you," said Miss Bristow. She smiled at Alison. "The usual."

Alison mixed the gin and vermouth for Miss Bristow with a kind of defeated disregard.

"I am feeling a bit shaky today," said Miss Bristow, slowly fitting herself into the chair and reaching for her drink. She sipped, gulped, sipped again, and said, "It was that film on the television about the mummy. They unwrapped it and I thought, 'Oh, my, I must turn this off.' But I couldn't. I just sat there while they unwrapped it. I thought, 'I know I'm going to have a bad night if I watch this' but I kept watching and they kept unwrapping. Finally, I couldn't stand it any more. I switched it off and went to bed. And I had a bad night."

"I didn't see it," said Philippa. "I was at a party. A publisher's thrash."

"It reminded me of something."

"The mummy?"

"Something else. A face I knew, a face from the catacombs — a long time ago."

"I didn't know you'd been in Rome."

"I have never been to Rome," said Miss Bristow.

Philippa looked at her watch. "I booked the table for one o'clock and the traffic's pretty bad. We ought to make a move."

"I'll just fetch my hat," said Miss Bristow. From the bedroom she heard Alison speaking to Philippa in a harsh accusing whisper.

* * *

"We've got lots to talk about," said Philippa in the restaurant. "And I have two ideas for you."

"Before you say another word," said Miss Bristow, pushing down her hat, "I want you to get that young man's attention and ask him for two drinks. There's a dear."

Philippa ordered the drinks and even began talking, but it was not until the gin and French was set before her that Miss Bristow's eyes lost their vacancy and took on a glaze of attention.

"I've been thinking," Philippa was saying, "that it's about

time you wrote your autobiography. I don't know why you haven't done it before! What an absolutely marvelous book it would be. Of course, I haven't mentioned it to Roger" — "Roger" to Philippa had been Mister Howlett to Miss Bristow for ten years — "but I know he'll be fantastically sweet about it."

"My autobiography?"

"Yes! It just occurred to me the other day," said Philippa. "I don't know how I thought of it! What do you say?"

Not one day of my life has gone by, Miss Bristow thought, without that book appearing to me. The book was constant, not as a mass of papers, but finished, a hefty lettered spine, occupying a thick space in a shelf in her mind.

She said, "It is a nice idea. But who would want to read it?"

"I certainly would!" said Philippa.

The girl was being unhelpful. Miss Bristow wanted more than this.

Philippa said, "London in the First World War, Paris in the twenties, London again — "

"My island," said Miss Bristow.

"Of course," said Philippa, but seemed disappointed.

"I haven't been back to Paris since 1938. It's such a long time ago. I wouldn't go back, not now. People say it's changed so much. I'd go back if I could do it — somehow — like being a fly on the wall, just watching and listening. But that's impossible. How can one be a fly on the wall? And my island. It wasn't what you might think. Some people think it was paradise — 'That beautiful life you must have had there,' they say. I say, 'What beautiful life?' "

"You could explain," said Philippa. "In the book."

"Montparnasse was small, too. It was a village. One knew everyone who lived there. I saw James Joyce. This was at a party. We spoke for a while, and I thought, 'What a kind man!' He had dark spectacles; he must have been nearly blind. I loved him — I don't think I even knew he was a writer —

and I felt that this was a man that one could depend on. *Dependable*, that's what I thought. Gertrude Stein was very noble — a very noble face. And there was Alice B."

"What did she do?" said Philippa.

"Knitting — something of the sort. Just sitting there and knitting, while Gertrude looked great and noble. I saw Hemingway — I didn't know him. But Djuna Barnes — how grand she looked! She had a huge cape on her shoulders, a huge black cape."

"So I was right!" said Philippa in triumph. "It will be a lovely book. I'm sure Roger will be thrilled. I don't know what gave me the idea, but I just knew it was a good one."

Miss Bristow smiled and put her glass down and pushed it until it hit the ashtray. Hearing the clink, Philippa looked down and then searched for the waiter. Fresh drinks were brought.

Miss Bristow said, "Once, at a party, I met the lunatic Crosby. He wanted to talk and he noticed I was wearing a pretty ring. This ring. 'I've been admiring your ring,' he said. 'The boy who gave me this ring just got out of prison,' I said."

Philippa lowered her head and frowned.

Miss Bristow said, "Crosby was very shocked. He looked at me and said, 'And you mean you kept it?' That's all he said. 'And you mean you kept it?' And he went away."

Philippa said, "That's just what I had in mind. Funnily enough, I never thought of James Joyce as dependable."

"I am telling you what I felt."

"It would be a marvelous book."

"What was the other thing?"

"What other thing?"

"You said you had two ideas," said Miss Bristow. "You have told me only one."

"Oh, yes," said Philippa. "Would you like another drink?"

"The same," said Miss Bristow.

Philippa's glass was full: one drink was brought. Miss Bristow sipped and watched Philippa trying to begin. The girl was having difficulty. Miss Bristow said, "Is it my new collection?"

"Partly. But first of all I want to tell you what a brilliant collection it is — "

With this preface, Miss Bristow thought, the news can only be bad. She was aware that it was an old woman's book, rather a monochrome, all memory, without adornment or invention. But Miss Bristow had discovered this as her strength.

Philippa was still praising her: the news was very bad.

Instead of speaking, Miss Bristow drank, and the drink was like speech, calming her, relieving the apprehension she felt, so that by the time the drink was gone and Philippa had finished, Miss Bristow was smiling and had forgotten her initial uneasiness about the girl's reservations. She heard herself saying, "Why, that's all right then, isn't it?"

"Gosh, you're quick." Philippa turned. Now the waiter was nearby and ready, anticipating the order. He brought Miss Bristow another drink.

"Lastly," said Philippa suddenly, surprising Miss Bristow. Miss Bristow peered over the rim of her glass.

"The icehouse story."

"Rather short, I'm afraid," said Miss Bristow.

"I have no objection to its length," said Philippa, looking very frightened.

"Does it seem overobvious to you?"

"Not that." The girl was lost. She looked around as if searching for a landmark and the right way through this confusion.

Miss Bristow said, "These waiters must be wondering what's keeping us."

Philippa took a deep breath and said, "Miss Bristow" — the name alone was warning of worse to come — "Miss Bristow, some of us at Howletts think it will hurt your reputation."

Saying so, Philippa sighed and squinted as if expecting the ceiling to crack and drop in pieces on her head.

Miss Bristow laughed hard at the girl in disbelief. And as she laughed she saw the people in the restaurant alter: they were skulls and bones and rags, and even Philippa was skeletal and sunken-eyed, with a zombie's stare.

"Who thinks that?" said Miss Bristow, spacing out her words.

"Roger — some others." Philippa used her teeth to clamp her lip and chafe it. "And I do, sort of. I mean, I can see their point."

"My reputation is no concern of mine. It is a figment in other people's imaginations. It does not belong to me. You should know that."

"I'm not sure I understand," said Philippa. "But I think I understand the icehouse story. It's easily one of the best-written things you've done, and maybe that's why I think it's going to hurt you."

"How can it possibly hurt me?"

Philippa said, "Well, it's anti-Negro for one thing."

"Yes?" Miss Bristow was incredulous; her eyes asked for more.

"And for another thing — " Philippa tried to go on, started twice, and finally said, "Isn't that enough?"

"If what you said were true it would, I suppose, be more than enough. But it is not true."

"It's what some readers will think."

"I don't care about 'some readers.' It's the others that I care about — and I do care, passionately."

"Roger thinks — "

"Tell me what you think," Miss Bristow said sharply.

"I think it presents the black people — oh, God, I hate people who say things like this, but anyway — I think it presents the black people in a bad light."

"It happened a long time ago," said Miss Bristow.

"Still — "

"Nineteen seventeen. The light could not have been worse."

"It worries me."

"Splendid. The story is a success."

"I'm sure it is," said Philippa. "Miss Bristow, would you like another drink?" Miss Bristow said she would appreciate a small one. Philippa said, "It seems racial."

"It is not about race. It is about condition."

Philippa said, "I hate to say this, but I think you should take it out."

Miss Bristow said, "It is true from start to finish. It is a memory. 'But they did not know that they were dying, like Romans becoming Italians' — the last line says it all. You are not interested, you do not want to know. Why won't you see?"

"You were so young then," said Philippa. "You might have been wrong."

Miss Bristow said, "I was about your age."

Philippa had not heard the sarcasm.

"But things are different now. You said so yourself."

"Did I say that?" Miss Bristow saw the faces — the dream skull, the one on the moving bus. And from a bus, on the street, six of them carrying placards, as savage seeming as long ago. She was not imagining those ghastly faces, the teeth, the red eyes, the dreadlocks. She said, "I have seen them."

And saw them now. The drink had come. She did not sip. She gulped from the glass, and spilled some.

Philippa said, "I feel terrible about this. Roger was fantastically sweet. Roger — "

In the restaurant, as in the dream and through the window, bony cheeks, dirty hair, and dusty bitten fingers. They were there, left and right, at the watery offside of her field of vision surrounding the men she saw; in shadow. They had swarmed like rats from the island and now they were here, lurking; they had gained entrance to this restaurant.

Miss Bristow said, "Perhaps you are right." She turned and no longer saw the ones in the corner. But there were others.

"Perhaps." They returned in their rags, but still she said, "You are right" and "Yes, yes," hoping the words would drive them away. Her agreement was merely ritual, like the effect of this glass: it made the fright worse but enabled her to bear it.

The young waiter hurried to Miss Bristow's side, as if instructed, and said, "The same again, madam?"

THE IMPERIAL
ICEHOUSE

OF ALL THE GRAND BUILDINGS on my island, the grandest by far was The Imperial Icehouse — white pillars and a shapely roof topped by ornate lettering on a gilded sign. Unlike the warehouses and the shops on the same street, it had no smell. It was whiter than the church, and though you would not mistake it for a church, the fresh paint and elongated windows — and the gold piping on the scrollwork of the sign — gave it at once a look of holiness and purpose. I cannot think of human endeavor without that building coming to mind, shimmering in my memory as it did on the island, the heat distorting it like its reflection in water.

The icehouse did more than cater to the comforts of the islanders. It provided ice for the fisherman's catch and the farmer's delicate produce. A famous Victorian novelist visited us in 1859 and remarked on it, describing it as "a drinking shop." It was certainly that, but it was more. It was "well attended" he said. He was merely passing through, a traveler interested in recording our eccentricities. He could not have known that The Imperial Icehouse was our chief claim to civilization. Ice in that climate! It was shipped to the island whole, and preserved. It was our achievement and our boast.

Then one day, decades later, four men came to town for a wagonload of ice. Three were black and had pretty names; the fourth was a white planter called Mr. Hand. He had made the trip with his Negroes because it was high summer and he wanted cold drinks. His plan was to carry away a ton of ice and store it in his estate upcountry. He was a new man on the island and had the strengths and weaknesses peculiar to all new arrivals. He was hard-working and generous; he talked a good deal about progress; he wore his eagerness on his face. He looked stunned and happy and energetic. He did not listen or conceal. On this the most British of the islands it was a satisfaction to newcomers to see the Victoria Statue on Victoria Street, and the horses in Hyde Park, and Nelson in Trafalgar Square. Mr. Hand saw no reason why he should not drink here as he had done in England.

He had taken over Martlet's estate, which had been up for sale ever since Martlet's death. That again revealed Mr. Hand as a newcomer, considering what had happened to old Martlet. And the estate was as far from town as it was possible to be on this island: Mr. Hand, a bachelor, must have needed consolation and encouragement.

He had, against all good advice, taken over the Martlet Negroes, and three of these accompanied him on that trip to town for the ice. Mr. Hand closed the deal at the icehouse by having a drink, and he sent a bucket of beer out to his men. They were called John Paul, Macacque, and Jacket. He had another drink, and another, and sent out more beer for those men who kept in the shade. It was not unlawful for Negro estate workers to drink in the daytime, but it was not the custom either. Even if he had known, Mr. Hand probably would not have cared.

The Negroes drank, conversing in whispers, shadows in shadow, accepting what they were offered, and waiting to be summoned to load the ice.

They had arrived in the coolness of early morning, but the drinking meant delay: by noon the wagon was still empty, the four horses still tethered to a tree, the Negroes sitting with their backs to the icehouse and their long legs stretched out. Perhaps the racket from inside told them there would be no hurry. In any case, they expected to leave at dusk, for not even the rankest newcomer would risk hauling ice across the island in the midafternoon heat.

Just as they had begun to doze, they were called. Mr. Hand stood and swayed on the verandah. He was ready, he yelled. He had to repeat it before his words were understood. Some other men came out of the icehouse and argued with him. Mr. Hand took them over to the wagon and showed them the sheets of canvas he had brought. He urged the men to watch as the Negroes swung the big wagon to the back door; and he supervised the loading, distributing sawdust between the great blocks of ice as if cementing for good the foundations of an imperial building.

For an hour or more the Negroes labored, two men to a cake, and Mr. Hand joked to them about it: Had they known water to be so heavy? An enormous block was winched from the door. John Paul, who was the leader of the three, withdrew an ice pick from his shirt and began to work its stiletto point on that block. There was a shout from Mr. Hand — again, the unexpected voice — and John Paul stood and patiently wiped the ice pick on his arm. When the block was loaded, the wheels were at a slant and the floor of the wagon had squashed the springs to such an extent that the planks rested on the axle trees. Mr. Hand continued to trowel the sawdust and separate the cakes with canvas until at last all the ice was loaded and the four horses hitched.

The news of the loading had reached the men drinking in the icehouse. A noisy crowd gathered on the verandah to watch the tipping wagon creak down Regent Street, Mr. Hand holding the reins, Macacque and Jacket tugging the bridles of the forward horses, John Paul sauntering at the rear.

Their progress was slow, and even before they disappeared past the tile kiln at the far end of the street many of the ice-house men had left the verandah to seek the cool bar.

Past the Wallace estate, and Villeneuve's dairy, the mile-stone at the flour mill; children had followed, but they too dropped back because of the heat. Others had watched from doorways, attracted by the size of the load and the rumble and wobble of the wheels in the rutted lanes. Now, no one fol-lowed.

There were no more houses. They had begun to climb the first range of hills. In this heat, on the exposed road, the birds were tiny and silent, and the flowers had no aroma. There was only a sawing of locusts and a smell of dust. From time to time, Jacket glimpsed the straining horse he held and looked over at Macacque, who frowned at the higher hills beyond.

The hills loomed; no one saw the hole in the road, only the toppling horses, the one behind Jacket rearing from a broken trace and free of one strap swinging himself and snapping an-other. Empty, the wagon had seemed secure; but this weight, and the shock of the sudden hole, made it shudder feebly and look as if it might burst. Jacket calmed the horse and quickly roped him. The others steadied the wagon.

Mr. Hand, asleep on his seat, had tumbled to his knees. He woke and swore at the men, then at the horses, and he cursed the broken straps. But he had more straps in the chest he had brought, and he was so absorbed in the repair he did not leave the road. He mended the traces — spurning the men's help — in the middle of the North Road, squinting in the sunshine.

They were soon on their way. There was a rime of froth on the necks and fetlocks of the horses, and great syrupy strings of yellow saliva dripped from their jaws. The road narrowed as it grew steep; then it opened again. The horses fought for footing and the wheels chimed as they banged against the wagon. The Negroes did not sing as they had on the early-morning ride, nor did they speak. Mr. Hand nodded, sat upright, slumped again, and was asleep.

Sensing the wagon slowing, John Paul put his shoulder under the back flap and gave a push. His shoulder was soaked; the wagon had begun to drip, dark pennies in the dust that dried almost as soon as they formed. He placed his forearms on the flap and put his head down and let the wagon carry him.

Passing the spring where they had stopped that morning for a drink, John Paul called out to Mr. Hand and asked if they could rest. No, said Mr. Hand, waking again and spreading his fingers to push at the sunlight. They would go on, he said; they were in a hurry. Now Jacket sang out — a brief squawking ditty, interrupting the silence of the hot road. He was answered by John Paul, another birdlike cry, and then Macacque's affirming gabble. John Paul took his ice pick and reached beneath the canvas. He chopped a wedge, and sucked it, then shared it with the two other Negroes. Mr. Hand gasped in sleep.

There was a cracking, a splintering of wood like a limb twisting from a tree. John Paul tossed his chunk of ice into the grass by the roadside, and he saw the rear wheel in pieces, a bunch of spokes settling under the wagon.

Glassy eyed from his nap, Mr. Hand announced to them that he had a spare wheel. He unbolted it from the bottom of the wagon and fitted it to the axle, but from where the others stood idle they could see that the ice had shifted and cracked the side boards. And yet, when the trip was resumed, the wagon rolled more smoothly, as if the load were lighter than before — the springs had bounce, the wheels were straighter.

More ice was chopped away by John Paul, and this he shared, and while Mr. Hand slept the three Negroes quarreled silently, sniffing and sighing, because John Paul had the ice pick and he would not let any of the others use it.

The road became bumpy again; the ice moved in the wagon. It had been securely roped, but now it was loose; it was a smaller load; its jarring woke Mr. Hand. He worked himself into a temper when he saw the diminished load. He stopped to tighten the canvas around it and screamed at the puddle that collected under the wagon. He would not let the Negroes drink. There will be cold drinks in plenty, he said, when we arrive home. Later, he got down from the seat on a steep grade and got behind and pushed with his shoulder like John Paul, and he said: That's how we do it.

They passed a fragrant valley. Negroes in that valley whispered and laughed and jeered at the Negroes in this procession. Now the ice was melting so quickly there was a stream of water pouring from the wagon and its cracks. The mockery was loud and several Negroes followed for some distance, yelling about the melting ice and the trail of mud they left through the pretty valley. The wagon wood was dark with moisture, as dark as the Negroes' faces, which were streaming with sweat.

Mr. Hand began to talk — crazy talk about England — and his men laughed at the pitch of his voice, which was a child's complaint. They did not understand his words; he ignored their laughter.

The left trace snapped as the right had done, a spoke worked loose and dropped from a wheel, although the wheel itself remained in position. One horse's shoe clanged as he kicked it into the belly of the wagon. These incidents were commented upon, and now the Negroes talked loudly of the stupidity of the trip, the waste of effort, the wrong time of day, the color of Mr. Hand's cheeks. Mr. Hand sat holding the reins loosely, his head tipped onto his shoulder. His straw hat fell off and the Negroes left it on the road where it fell. John Paul looked back and saw his footprint crushed into the crown.

They had gained the second range of hills, and descending — slowly, so that the wagon would not be shot forward — the late-afternoon sun, unshielded by any living tree, struck their faces like metal. The road was strewn with boulders on which the horses did a tired dance, stepping back. There was a curve, another upward grade, and at that corner the horses paused to crop the grass.

There was no sound from Mr. Hand. He was a crouching infant in his seat, in the sun's glare, his mouth open. The horses tore at the grass with their lips. The Negroes crept under the wagon, and there they stayed in the coolness, for an hour or more, the cold water dripping on them.

Mr. Hand woke, stamping his feet on the planks. They scrambled to their places.

His anger was exhausted in three shouts. He promised them ice, cold drinks, a share for everyone, and as he spoke the Negroes could see how the ice beneath the sagging canvas was a quarter the size of what it had been. Divided, it would be nothing. They did not respond to Mr. Hand's offer: it was a promise of water, which they had already as their right, from their own spring.

Mr. Hand tugged the reins and the men helped the horses, dragged the wagon, dragged the ice, dragged this man through the tide of heat. Mr. Hand chattered, repeating his promises, but when he saw the impassive faces of the Negroes he menaced them with whining words. He spoke sharply, like an insect stirred by the sun.

If you don't pull hard, he said to the men, I'll free the horses and hitch you to the wagon — and you'll take us home. He thwacked the canvas with his whip. There was no thud, nothing solid, only a thin echoless smack, and he clawed open the canvas. Shrunken ice blocks rattled on the planks.

He stopped the wagon and leaped out and faced each man in turn and accused him. The men did nothing; they waited for him to move. And he did. He hit Macacque and called him a thief. Jacket was lazy, he said, and he hit him. John Paul prepared himself for worse. Mr. Hand came close to him and screamed and, as he did, the wagon lurched. The horses had found grass: they pulled the wagon to the roadside.

The sounds of the horses chewing, the dripping of the wagon in the heat; it was regular, like time leaking away. Mr. Hand raised his whip and rushed at John Paul. And then, in that low sun, Mr. Hand cast three shadows; two helped him aside, and he struggled until a sound came, the sound John Paul had made in town with his ice pick, like ice being chipped, or bone struck, and the hatless man cried out — plea, promise, threat, all at once — and staggered to the wagon and shouted at the water dripping into the dust. The ice was no larger than a man, and bleeding in the same way.

At last it was cool and dark and they were passing the first fences of the farm and turning into the drive. There were lighted huts and lights moving toward them, swinging tamely on nothing in the darkness. Voices near those lanterns cried out — timid questions. The three men answered in triumph from the top of the heavy wagon, which rumbled in the road like a broken catafalque, streaming, still streaming, though all the ice was gone.

YARD SALE

As things turned out, Floyd had no choice but to spend the summer with me in East Sandwich. To return home to find his parents divorced was awkward; but to learn that they had already held their yard sale was distinctly shaming. I had been there and seen my sister's ghastly jollity as she disposed of her old Hoover and shower curtains and the chair she had abandoned caning; Floyd senior, with a kind of hostile generosity, turned the whole affair into a potlatch ceremony by bestowing his power tools on his next-door neighbor and clowning among his junk with the word "freebie." "Aunt Freddy can have my life jacket," he crowed. "I'm not your aunt," I said, but I thanked him for it and sent it via the local church to Bangladesh, where I hoped it would arrive before the monsoon hit Chittagong. After the yard sale, they made themselves scarce — Floyd senior to his Boston apartment and his flight attendant, my sister to the verge of a nervous breakdown in Cuttyhunk. I was glad to be deputized to look after little Floyd, and I knew how relieved he would be, after two years in the Peace Corps in Western Samoa, to have some home cooking and the sympathetic ear of his favorite aunt. He, too, would be burdened and looking for buyers.

At Hyannis Airport, I expected a waif, an orphan of sorts,

with a battered suitcase and a heavy heart. But Floyd was all
smiles as he peered out of the fuselage, and when the steps
were lowered and he was on them, the little plane actually
rocked to and fro: Floyd had gained seventy-five pounds. A
Henry Moore muppet of raw certainty, he was dark, with hair
like varnished kapok and teeth gleaming like Chiclets. He
wore an enormous shirt printed with bloated poppies, and the
skirtlike sarong that Margaret Mead tells us is called a *lava-
lava*. On his feet were single-thong flip-flops, which, when he
kicked them off — as he did in the car, to sit cross-legged on
the bucket seat — showed his toes to be growing in separate
directions.

"Wuppertal," he said, or words to that effect. There was
about him a powerful aroma of coconut oil and a rankness of
dead leaves and old blossoms.

"Greetings," I said.

"That's what I just said."

"And welcome home."

"It doesn't seem like home anymore."

We passed the colonial-style (rough-hewn logs, split-rail
fence, mullion windows) Puritan Funeral Home, Kopper
Krafts, the pizza joints, and it occurred to me that this part of
Route 132 had changed out of all recognition. I thought: Poor
kid.

The foreknowledge that I would be led disloyally into loose
talk about his father's flight attendant kept me silent about his
parents' divorce. I asked him about Samoa; I was sure he was
aching to be quizzed. This brought from him a snore of approval and a native word. I mentioned his sandals.

He said, "My mother never wears sandals. She's always
barefoot!"

I determined upon delicacy. "It's been a hard year."

"She says the craziest things sometimes."

"Nerves."

Here was the Hyannis Drive-In Movie. I was going to point
out to him that while he had been away, they had started hold-

ing drive-in church services on Sunday mornings — an odd contrast to Burt Reynolds in the evenings, the sacred and the profane in the same amphitheatre. But Floyd was talking about his father.

"He's amazing, and what a sailor! I've known him to go out in a force-nine gale. He's completely reckless."

Aren't the young downright? I thought. I did not say anything about the life jacket his old man had given me; I was sure he had done it out of malice, knowing full well that what I had really coveted was the dry pinewood sink lost in the potlatch.

"Floyd," I said, with a shrill note of urgency in my voice — I was frantic to drag him off the topic I knew would lead him to his parents' fractured marriage — "what about Samoa?"

"Sah-moa," he said, moving his mouth like a chorister as he corrected my pronunciation. So we have an emphatic stammer on the first syllable, do we? I can take any amount of well-intentioned pedantry, but I draw the line at condescension from someone I have laboriously diapered. It was so difficult for me to mimic this unsayable word that I countered with "And yet, I wonder how many of them would get Haverhill right?"

Floyd did not move from his Buddha posture. "Actually, he's wicked right-wing, and very moralistic about things. I mean, deep down. He hates change of any kind."

"You're speaking of — ?"

"My father."

Your psychiatrists say grief is a great occasion for rationalizing. Still, the Floyd senior I knew was indiscernible through this coat of whitewash. He was the very engine of change. Though my sentence was fully framed, I didn't say to his distracted son, That is a side of your father I have not been privileged to observe.

"Mother's different."

"How so?"

"Confident. Full of beans. Lots of savvy."

And beside herself in Cuttyhunk. Perhaps we do invent the friends and even the parents we require, and yet I was not quite prepared for what Floyd said next.

"My sister's pretty incredible, too. I've always thought of myself as kind of athletic, but she can climb trees twice as fast as me."

This was desperate: he had no sister. Floyd was an only child. I had an overwhelming desire to slap his face, as the hero does in B movies to bring the flannel-mouthed fool to his senses.

But he had become effusive. "My sister . . . my brother . . . my grandmother" — inventing a fictitious family to make up for the one that had collapsed in his absence.

I said, "Floyd dear, you're going to think your old auntie is horribly literal-minded, but I don't recognize your family from anything you've said. Oh, sure, I suppose your father *is* conservative — the roué is so often a puritan underneath it all. And vice versa. Joseph Smith? The Mormon prophet? What was it, fifty wives? 'When I see a pretty girl, I have to pray,' he said. *His* prayers were answered! But listen, your mother's had a dreadful time. And, um, you don't actually have any brothers or sisters. Relax. I know we're under a little strain, and absolutely bursting with Samoa, but — "

"In Samoa," he said, mocking me with the half sneeze of its correct pronunciation, "it's the custom to join a local family. You live with them. You're one of them."

"Much as one would join the Elks around here?"

"It's wicked complicated."

"More Masonic — is that it?"

"More Samoan. You get absorbed kind of. They prefer it that way. And they're very easygoing. I mean, there's no word for bastard in Samoan."

"With so little traffic on the roads, there's probably no need for it. Sorry. I see your point. But isn't that taking the extended family a bit far? What about your parents?"

"He thatches roofs and she keeps chickens."

"Edith and Floyd senior?"

"Oh, them" was all he said.

"But you've come home!"

"I don't know. Maybe I just want to find my feet."

Was it his turn of phrase? I dropped my eyes and saw a spider clinging to his ankle. I said, "Floyd, don't move — there's a creature on your foot."

He pinched it lovingly. "It's only a tattoo."

That seemed worse than a live spider, which had the merit of being able to dance away. I told him this, adding, "Am I being fastidious?"

"No, ethnocentric," he said. "My mother has a mango on her knee."

"Not a banjo?" When I saw him wince, I said, "Forgive me, Floyd. Do go on — I want to hear everything."

"There's too much to tell."

"I know the feeling."

"I wouldn't mind a hamburger," he said suddenly. "I'm starving."

Instead of telling him I had cassoulet waiting for him in East Sandwich, I slowed down. It is the fat, not the thin, who are always famished; and he had not had a hamburger in two years. But the sight of fast food woke a memory in him. As he watched the disc of meat slide down a chute to be bunned, gift wrapped, and clamped into a small styrofoam valise, he treated me to a meticulous description of the method of cooking in Samoa. First, stones were heated, he said, then the hot stones buried in a hole. The uncooked food was wrapped in leaves and placed on the stones. More hot stones were piled on top. Before he got to the part where the food, stones, and leaves were disinterred, I said, "I understand that's called labor intensive, but it doesn't sound terribly effective."

He gave me an odd look and excused himself, taking his little valise of salad to the drinking fountain to wash it.

"We always wash our food before we eat."

I said, "Raccoons do that!"

It was meant as encouragement, but I could see I was not doing at all well.

Back at the house, Floyd dug a present out of his bag. You sat on it, this fiber mat. "One of your miracle fibers?" I said. "Tell me more!" But he fell silent. He demurred when I mentioned tennis, and at my suggestion of an afternoon of recreational shopping he grunted. He said, "We normally sleep in the afternoon." Again I was a bit startled by the plural pronoun and glanced around, half expecting to see another dusky islander. But no — Floyd's was the brotherly folk "we" of the native, affirming the cultural freemasonry of all Polynesia. And it had clearly got into his bones. He had acquired an almost catlike capacity for slumber. He lay for hours in the lawn hammock, swinging like a side of beef, and at sundown entered the house yawning and complaining of the cold. It was my turn to laugh: the thermometer on the deck showed eighty-one degrees.

"I'll bet you wish you were at Trader Vic's," I said over the cassoulet, trying to avert my ethnocentric gaze as Floyd nibbled the beans he seized with his fingers. He turned my Provençal cuisine into a sort of astronaut's pellet meal.

He belched hugely, and guessing that this was a ritual rumble of Samoan gratitude, I thanked him.

"Ironic, isn't it?" I said. "You seem to have managed marvelously out there in the Pacific, taking life pretty much as you found it. And I can't help thinking of Robert Louis Stevenson, who went to Samoa with his sofas, his tartans, his ottoman, and every bagpipe and ormolu clock from Edinburgh in his luggage."

"How do you know that?" he asked.

"Vassar," I said. "There wasn't any need for Stevenson to join a Samoan family. Besides his wife and his stepson, there were his stepdaughter and her husband. His wife was a divorcée, but she was from California, which explains everything. Oh, he brought his aged mother out, too. She never stopped starching her bonnets, so they say."

"Tusitala," said Floyd.

"Come again?"

"That was his title. 'Teller of tales.' He read his stories to the Samoans."

"I'd love to know what they made of 'Weir of Hermiston.' " It was clear from Floyd's expression that he had never heard of the novel.

He said gamely, "I didn't finish it."

"That's not surprising — neither did Stevenson. Do much reading, Floyd?"

"Not a lot. We don't have electricity, and reading by candlelight is really tough."

" 'Hermiston' was written by candlelight. In Samoa. It would be an act of the greatest homage to the author to read it that way."

"I figured it was pointless to read about Samoa if you live there."

"All the more reason to read it, since it's set in eighteenth-century Scotland."

"And he was a *palagi*."

"Don't be obscure, Floyd."

"A white man."

Only in the sense that Pushkin was an octoroon and Othello a soul brother, I thought, but I resisted challenging Floyd. Indeed, his saturation in the culture had made him indifferent to the bizarre. I discovered this when I drew him out. What was the food like after it was shoveled from beneath the hot stones? On Floyd's report it was uninspired: roots, leaves, and meat, sweated together in this subterranean sauna. What kind of meat? Oh, all kinds; and with the greatest casualness he let it drop that just a week before, he had eaten a flying fox.

"On the wing?" I asked.

"They're actually bats," he said. "But they call them — "

"Do you mean to tell me that you have eaten a bat?"

"You act as if it's an endangered species," he said.

"I should think Samoans are if that's part of their diet."

"They're not bad. But they cook them whole, so they always have a strange expression on their faces when they're served."

"Doesn't surprise me a bit. Turn up their noses, do they?"

"Sort of. You can see all their teeth. I mean, the bats'."

"What a stitch!"

He smiled. "You think that's interesting?"

"Floyd, it's matchless."

Encouraged, he said, "Get this — we use fish as fertilizer. Fish!"

"That's predictable enough," I said, unimpressed. "Not far from where you are now, simple folk put fresh fish on their vegetable gardens as fertilizer. Misguided? Maybe. Wasteful? Who knows? Such was the nature of subsistence farming on the Cape three hundred years ago. One thing, though — they knew how to preach a sermon. Your agriculturalist is so often a God-fearing man."

This cued Floyd into an excursion on Samoan Christianity, which sounded to me thoroughly homespun and basic, full of a good-natured hypocrisy that took the place of tolerance.

I said, "That would make them — what? Unitarians?"

Floyd belched again. I thanked him. He wiped his fingers on his shirtfront and said it was time for bed. He was not used to electric light: the glare was making him belch. "Besides, we always go to bed at nine."

The hammering some minutes later was Floyd rigging up the hammock in the spare room, where there was a perfectly serviceable double bed.

"We never do," I called.

*   *   *

FLOYD looked so dejected at breakfast, toying with his scrambled egg and sausage, that I asked him if it had gone cold. He shrugged. Everything was hunky-dory, he said in Samoan, and then translated it.

"What do you normally have for breakfast?"

"Taro."

"Is it frightfully good for you?"

"It's a root," he said.

"Imagine finding your roots in Samoa!" Seeing him darken, I added, "Carry on, Floyd. I find it all fascinating. You're my window on the world."

But Floyd shut his mouth and lapsed into silence. Later in the morning, seeing him sitting cross-legged in the parlor, I was put in mind of one of those big lugubrious animals that look so homesick behind the bars of American zoos. I knew I had to get him out of the house.

It was a mistake to take him to the supermarket, but this is hindsight; I had no way of anticipating his new fear of traffic, his horror of crowds, or the chilblains he claimed he got from air conditioning. The acres of packaged foods depressed him, and his reaction to the fresh-fruit department was extraordinary.

"One fifty-nine!" he jeered. "In Samoa, you can get a dozen bananas for a penny. And look at that," he said, handling a whiskery coconut. "They want a buck for it!"

"They're not exactly in season here on the Cape, Floyd."

"I wouldn't pay a dollar for one of those."

"I had no intention of doing so."

"They're dangerous, coconuts," he mused. "They drop on your head. People have been known to be killed by them."

"Not in Barnstable County," I said, which was a pity, because I felt like aiming one at his head and calling it an act of God.

He hunched over a pyramid of oranges, examining them with distaste and saying that you could buy the whole lot for a quarter in a village market he knew somewhere in remote Savai'i. A tray of mangoes, each fruit the rich color of old meerschaum, had Floyd gasping with contempt: the label stuck to their skins said they were two dollars apiece, and he had never paid more than a nickel for one.

"These cost two cents," he said, bruising a grapefruit with his thumb, "and they literally give these away," he went on, flinging a pineapple back onto its pile. But his disbelief was nothing compared to the disbelief of shoppers, who gawped at his *lava-lava*. Yet his indignation at the prices won these people over, and amid the crashing of carts I heard the odd shout of "Right on!"

Eventually I hauled him away, and past the canned lychees ("They grow on trees in China, Floyd!") I became competitive. "What about split peas?" I said, leading him down the aisles. "Scallops? Indian pudding? Dreft? Clorox? What do you pay for dog biscuits? Look, be reasonable. What you gain on mangoes, you lose on maple syrup!"

We left empty-handed. Driving back, I noticed that Floyd had become even gloomier. Perhaps he realized that it was going to be a long summer. I certainly did.

"Anything wrong, Floyd?"

He groaned. He put his head in his hands. "Aunt Freddy, I think I've got culture shock."

"Isn't that something you get at the other end? I mean, when the phones don't work in Nigeria or you find ants in the marmalade or the grass hut leaks?"

"Our huts never leak."

"Of course not," I said. "And look, this is only a *palagi* talking, but I have the unmistakable feeling that you would be much happier among your own family, Floyd."

We both knew which family. Mercifully, he was gone the next day, leaving nothing behind but the faint aroma of coconut oil in the hammock. He never asked where I got the price of the Hyannis-Apia airfare. He accepted it with a sort of extortionate Third Worlder's wink, saying, "That's very Samoan of you, Aunt Freddy." But I'll get it back. Fortunately, there are ways of raising money at short notice around here.

ALGEBRA

RONALD HAD THREATENED to move out before, but I always begged him not to. He knew he had power over me. He was one of those people who treats flattery as if it is mockery, and regards insult as a form of endearment. You couldn't talk to him. He refused to be praised, and if I called him "Fanny" he only laughed. I suppose he knew that basically he was worthless, which led him to a kind of desperate boasting about his faults — he even boasted about his impotence. What Ronnie liked best was to get drunk on the cheap wine he called "Parafino" and sprawl on the chaise and dig little hornets out of his nose and say what scum most people were. I knew he was bad for me and that I would have another breakdown if things went on like this much longer.

"God's been awful good to me," he said once in the American accent he affected when he was drunk.

"That's blasphemy," I said. "You don't mean that. You'll go to Hell."

"Wrong!" he shrieked. "If you *do* mean it you'll go to Hell."

When I met him he had just joined Howletts, the publisher. Quite early on, he began to sneer at the parties he sometimes took me to by boasting that he could go to one every day of the week. I thought he had a responsible position but afterwards, when I got to know the others, particularly Philippa and Roger, I came to realize that he was a rather insignificant person in the firm. I think this is why he seemed so embarrassed to have me along and took me so seldom. He implied that I wasn't attractive or intelligent enough for his publishing friends, and he would not let me near the real writers.

"This is Michael Insole, a friend," he'd say, never letting on that we were living together in my flat. That sort of thing left me feeling incredibly depressed.

Then everything changed. I have not really analyzed it until now. It certainly wasn't an idea — nothing as solemn or calculated as that. It was more an impulse, a frenzy you might say, or a leap in the dark. At one of the parties I was talking to Sir Charles Moonman, the novelist and critic. "And what do you do?" he asked me. At another time I might have said, "I live with Ronald Brill," but I was feeling so fed up with Ronnie I said, "Basically, I'm a writer."

"Do I know your work?" asked Sir Charles.

"No," I said. It was the truth. I worked then, as I do now, at the Arcade Off-License near the Clapham South tube station, but living with Ronnie had made me want to go into writing.

Sir Charles found my prompt reply very funny, and then an odd thing happened. He relaxed and began to talk and talk. He was hugely old and had the downright manner and good health of a country doctor. He was reading Kingsley, he said, and squeezed air with his hands. He described the book, but it was nothing like any Kingsley I had ever read. He said, "It has, don't you agree, just the right tone, an elasticity one associates with fiction — " I nodded and tried to add something of my own, but could not get a word in.

At this point, Virginia Byward, the novelist and traveler, ambled over and said hello.

"This is Mister Insole. He's a writer," said Sir Charles. "We've just been talking about Kinglake."

Kinglake, not Kingsley. I was glad I had not said anything.

"*Eothen?* That Kinglake?" said Miss Byward.

"*The Invasion of the Crimea.* That Kinglake," said Sir Charles.

"Well, I'll let you two get on with it," said Miss Byward, laughing at her mistake. "Very nice to have met you, Mister Insole."

"She's so sweet," said Sir Charles. "And her reportage is devastating." He clawed at his cuff. "Bother. It's gone eight. I must rush — dinner engagement."

"I'll be late for mine, as well," I said. "My hostess will tear a strip off me." But I was not going anywhere.

"Such a bore, isn't it?" he said. "We are both being called away. So unfortunate. I would much rather stand and chat about the Crimean War."

"So would I!" I said. Then, I could think of nothing else to say, so I said, "I am one of your most passionate fans."

This was my leap in the dark. I had never read a word he had written. I suppose I looked terrified, but you would not have known it from the look on Sir Charles's face — pure joy. He removed his pipe from his mouth and stuffed his finger in the bowl.

"I'm so glad."

"I'm not joking," I said. "I find your work a real consolation. It genuinely engages me."

"It is awfully good of you to say so."

He sounded as if he meant it. More than that, he reacted as if no one had ever said these words to him before.

"We must meet for lunch one day." He clenched the pipe stem in his teeth and beamed.

I said, "How about dinner at my place? When you're free."

And Sir Charles Moonman, the eminent novelist and critic, said to me, "I am free most evenings."

"Next week?"

"I can do Monday, or Tuesday, or — "

"Monday," I said. I gave him my address and that was that.

He clapped me on the shoulder in his bluff country doctor way, and I was still somewhat dazed when Ronald came over.

"What are you grinning about?"

"I've just invited Sir Charles Moonman for dinner."

Ronald was horrified. "You can't," he said. "I'll phone him in the morning and tell him it's off."

"You'll do no such thing," I said, raising my voice to a pitch that had Ronald shushing me and steering me to a corner.

"What are you going to give him?"

He had me there. I do a nice shepherd's pie, and Ronald had often praised my flan, but truly I had not given the menu much thought, and told him so.

"Shepherd's pie!" Ronald was saying as Virginia Byward sidled up to me.

"Hello, Mister Insole," she said. She had remembered my name! "Has Charles gone?"

Ronald was speechless.

"Charles had to be off," I said. "A dinner party — he was rather dreading it."

Miss Byward was staring at Ronald.

"I know Mister Insole is a writer," she said. "But what do you do?"

Ronald turned purple. He said, "I sell worthless books," and marched away.

"I hope I didn't say anything to offend him," said Miss Byward. "Too bad about Charles. I was hoping he'd still be here. I meant to lock horns with him."

"If you're free on Monday, come along for dinner. Charles will be there."

"I couldn't crash your dinner party."

"Be my guest," I said. "It won't be fancy, but I think of myself as a good plain cook."

"If you're sure it's no trouble — "

"I'd be honored," I said, and then I could think of nothing to say except, "I am one of your most passionate fans," the statement that had gone down so well with Sir Charles. I was a bit embarrassed about saying it, because repeating it made it sound formulated and insincere. But it was my embarrassment that brought it off.

"Are you?" she said. She was clearly delighted.

"Your reportage is devastating."

It was as easy as twisting a tap. I said nothing more. I simply listened to her talk, and finally she said, "I've so enjoyed our little chat. See you Monday."

Ronald was silent on the way home until we got to Kennington or The Oval. Then he said, "Are you a writer?"

At Stockwell, I said, "Are you a publisher?"

As the train drew into Clapham Common, he stood up and said, "You're shameless." He pushed past me and ran up the escalator.

That night Ronald slept on the chaise and the next day he moved out of the flat and out of my life.

* * *

I had not known how easy it would be to make the acquaintance of Sir Charles Moonman and Miss Byward. It had only been necessary to learn a new language, and it was one that Ronald either despised or did not know. When I went broody about Ronald's absence over the weekend I remembered the guests I'd invited for Monday and I cheered up.

But on Sunday I began to worry about the numbers. Three people did not seem much of a dinner party and I kept hearing myself saying, "I like the intimate sort of party." So I invited Mr. Momma, too. Mr. Momma, a Cypriot, was a house painter who lived in the top-floor flat. He never washed his milk bottles, so Ronald had named him "Inky," which was short for "inconsiderate." Mr. Momma said he would do a salad.

On Monday I went to the library and got copies of Sir Charles's and Miss Byward's books. I was setting them out, arranging them on tables, when the phone rang. I must have been feeling a bit insecure still because I thought at once that it was either Sir Charles or Miss Byward who had rung to say they couldn't make it after all.

"Michael?"

It was Tanya Moult, one of Ronald's authors. I should say one of Ronald's victims, because he had strung her along for years. She was working on a book about pirates, women pirates, and Ronald had said it was just the ticket, a kind of robust woman's thing. That was very Ronald. He had other people doing books on cowboys — black cowboys; hairdressers and cooks — all men; gay heroes, and cats in history. Tanya sent him chapters and at the same time she scraped a living writing stories for women's magazines under a pseudonym. Ronald was very possessive about Tanya, but perversely so: he kept me away from her while at the same time being nasty to her.

I told her that Ronald had moved out. It was the first she had heard of it and I could tell that she was really down. Ronald had not been in touch with her about her newest chapter.

"Look, Tanya," I said — it was the first time I had used her Christian name. "Why don't you come round tonight? I'm having a few friends over for dinner."

She hesitated. I knew what she was thinking — I couldn't blame her.

"Sir Charles Moonman," I said. "And Virginia Byward."

"Gosh, Michael, really?"

"And Mister Momma from upstairs."

"I've met him," she said. "I don't know whether I have anything to wear."

"Strictly informal. If I know Sir Charles he'll be wearing an old cardigan, and Virginia will be in a rather shapeless tunic."

She said she would be there. At seven, Mr. Momma appeared in a bulging blue jumpsuit, carrying plastic bags of lettuce and onions and some tubs of dressing. He said, "How do you know I like parties?" and pulled one bulge out of his pocket — an avocado. His teeth were big, one was cracked, he wore a gold crucifix on a chain around his neck, and he smelled of sweat and soap. He sniffed. "Cooking food!" He swung his bags onto the table. "Salad," he said. "I make fresh. Like my madder."

I had never seen Mr. Momma happier. He shooed me out of the kitchen and then busied himself chopping and grating, and whistling through the crack in his tooth.

Tanya arrived on the dot of eight with a bottle of Hungarian Riesling. "I'm so excited," she said, and I realized just how calm I was. The bell rang again.

"Oh, my God," cried Mr. Momma.

Tanya went to the kitchen door and smiled.

"Like my madder," Mr. Momma said.

Sir Charles was breathless when I met him on the landing.

"I should have warned you about those stairs," I said.

But his breathlessness helped. He was panting, as if he had been cornered after a long chase and he could do nothing but smile and gasp his thanks as he was introduced to Tanya. He found a chair and propelled himself backward into it and sighed.

"Wine?" I said.

"That would be lovely."

I poured him a glass of Montrachet, gave him its pedigree (but omitted the fact that I had got it at a staff discount from Arcade Off-License) and left him to Tanya.

" — it's not generally known, but there were a fantastic number," Tanya was saying, and she was off: women pirates. Sir Charles was captivated.

"Do you know," said Virginia Byward when she arrived, glancing around the flat and relaxing at the sight of two copies of her books, "this is only the second time in my life I've been to Clapham? I'd rather not talk about the first time. I came a cropper that night!" She spoke to Sir Charles: "It was during the war."

"Something for your biographer," said Sir Charles.

We all laughed at this. But I thought then, and I continued to think throughout the evening, that I was now a part of their lives and that the time they were spending with me mattered. Each great writer seems to me to contain a posthumous book, the necessary and certain biography. Writers carry this assurance of posterity around with them. This was a page of that book.

This: my chaise, on which Miss Byward was sitting; my brass Benares ashtray with a smoldering thimble shape of Sir Charles's pipe tobacco in it; my tumbling tradescancia; my gate-legged dining table on which one of Ronald's dents was still visible; my footstool with its brocade cushion; my crystal sugar bowl; the wine glass Miss Byward was holding; the pillow Tanya was hugging; my basketwork fruit holder; me.

I excused myself and went into the kitchen. Mr. Momma was putting the finishing touches to his salad. He had made a little hill of chopped lettuce leaves and sprinkled it with olives and pimentoes and drips of dressing.

"You love it?"

I said it was perfect.

"It is a woman's tee-tee," he said, and made a knob-turning gesture with his hand.

In the parlor, my other guests were engrossed in conversation. I thought they were talking about an author they all respected; a name seemed to repeat (*Murray? Gilbert Murray?*). I pretended to straighten the leg of the table so I could get the drift of their conversation, but I quickly grasped that they were talking about money. (And I heard myself saying on a future occasion, *I thought they were talking about an author they all respected . . .*)

"I don't know how some people manage," said Sir Charles.

"I really don't. By the way, Michael, this wine is superb. You didn't tell me you had a cellar."

"I have an attic too," I said.

"Isn't he a poppet!" said Virginia.

Mr. Momma brought out his salad.

"Bravo," said Virginia, and hearing Mr. Momma's accent, she asked him where he was from. His mention of Cyprus had Virginia asking him which particular village was his and brought a long very practiced-sounding story from Sir Charles about a hotel in Limassol. Throughout the meal we talked intimately about Lawrence Durrell and I even found myself chipping in every now and then. I could see that it was considered quite a coup to have Mr. Momma on hand.

"And what is our friend from Cyprus doing in London?" asked Virginia.

"I am a painter."

Mr. Momma did not have the English to amplify this. He was quickly taken to be a tormented artist in exile rather than the hard-working house painter he was. We talked about the Mediterranean sense of color, and afterward Mr. Momma ran upstairs for his Cypriot records. He played them, he danced with Virginia, and he told her he loved her. Then he sat down and sobbed into his handkerchief.

"I've been admiring this wine glass," said Virginia over Mr. Momma's muted hoots. "Is it part of a set?"

I said, "Just the one," and filled it with the claret I had brought out for the shepherd's pie.

I was relieved when Sir Charles said he had to go, because that was my signal to open the Krug, which went down a treat. Then Sir Charles and Virginia shared a taxi back to Hampstead and Tanya (making a crack about Ronald) said she had never enjoyed herself more. Hearing what Tanya had said, Mr. Momma put his arm around me. He smelled strenuously of his dancing.

"No," I said, and led him to the door. "Let's not spoil it."

I slept alone, but I was not alone. The evening had been a great success. Both Sir Charles and Virginia sent me notes, thanking me for having them. They were brief notes, but I replied saying that the pleasure had been all mine.

Afterward, I wondered why they had agreed to come. I decided that their very position had something to do with it. They were so grand that most people thought that they must be very busy, so no one dared to invite them. And people believed that they were beyond praise. But my flattery, my offer of a meal, my discount wines had done the trick.

I had worked hard to make the evening festive, and Mr. Momma had been an unexpected success. And what had I asked of them? Nothing — nothing but for them to be there.

I had told them I was a writer. Because I had said this no one talked about it: I was one of them. Anyway, a good host is preoccupied with managing his party. His graciousness is silence when it is not encouragement. He isn't supposed to say much, only to keep the dishes coming and the glasses filled. So, in the end, they did not know much about me. They talked to each other.

The proof that Miss Byward meant what she said about enjoying herself was her invitation to me several weeks later for drinks at her very tiny flat in Hampstead. It was not until I saw her flat that I fully understood how she could have seen something to admire in mine. She was clearly an untidy person, but I was grateful when she introduced me as "Michael Insole, the writer." There were six others there, all writers whose names I instantly recognized, but because of the seating arrangements, I had no choice but to talk to Wibbert the poet. He told me a very entertaining story about giving a poetry reading in Birmingham, and he finished by saying, "The pay's appalling. They always apologize when they hand it over."

Henry Wibbert was a tall balding youth with the trace of a regional accent, and bitten fingernails, something I had always hated until I met him. His socks had slipped into his shoes and I could see his white ankles. His poet's love of failure was written all over him, and when I told him I did not write poetry he seemed to take this as a criticism — as if I were acting superior — and I wanted to tell him that, in fact, I had never written anything at all.

"I do the odd spot of reviewing," he said, somewhat defensively. And then, "I can always go back to teaching yobboes if I find myself really hard up." He twisted his finger into his mouth and chewed. "I'm sure your earnings have you in the supertax bracket."

"Far from it," I said. "I find it very hard to manage."

At once, he was friendlier. We had found common ground as struggling writers.

"It's hand to mouth with me," he said.

I said, "I was having this very conversation with Sir Charles Moonman just the other night."

"He hasn't got my worries," said Wibbert, though when I had said Sir Charles's name Wibbert looked closely at me, the way a person peers from a high window to an interesting spectacle below.

"You'd be surprised."

"If it was a struggle for that pompous overpraised old bastard?" he said. "Yes, I'd be very surprised."

"Have you ever met him?"

Wibbert shook his head.

"Why don't you come over some evening? You might change your mind."

Wibbert said, "He'd probably hate me."

"Absolutely not," I said.

"How can you be so sure?"

"Because I'm sure he's read your poetry, and if he has how could he fail to be an admirer of yours?"

This did the trick. Wibbert wrote his telephone number on the back of my hand in ballpoint, and as he had to hold my hand in his in order to do this it was noticed by the others at Miss Byward's as a rather eloquent gesture.

"You're not leaving," said Miss Byward, when I asked for my cape.

"A dinner engagement. Unfortunately. I would so much rather stay here and chat. It's been lovely."

She released me and afterward I wondered whether she had not said those very words to me. On the bus home I thought how much more satisfying it was to be a host than a guest.

I went home and after four tries typed a letter to Sir Charles, which I copied out in longhand — I liked the look of spontaneous intimacy in a handwritten letter. I was sure he would appreciate it. I told him about Wibbert and said that Wibbert was dead keen to meet him, if we could fix a day.

The reply from Sir Charles came in the form of an invitation from the Royal Society of Literature in which I was named as his guest at a lecture by Cyril Crowder on "Our Debt to Hugh Walpole." Although a reply was not requested I dashed off a note to the Society's secretary and said I'd be delighted to attend. And another to Sir Charles. On the day, I was so impatient I arrived early and chatted to the only person I could find, a little old lady fussing at a table. I had very nearly invited her to meet Sir Charles when she revealed herself as one of the tea ladies and said, "I should have a cream bun now if I was you. They're always the first to go."

Just before the lecture the room filled with people, Sir Charles among them. I blushed when a man, on being introduced to me by Sir Charles, said yes, indeed, he knew my work well. Sir Charles was pleased, and so was I, but I quickly took myself to a corner of the room. Here, a group of people were talking to a man who was obviously the center of attention. I made a beeline for this man, but instead of speaking, simply listened to what the others were saying. The man smiled at me a number of times.

"His friendship with James amounted to influence," someone said. "I believe it was very great."

"Deep," said the man, and smiled at me.

I swallowed my fear and said, "Profound."

"That's it," said the man and thanked me with his eyes.

"They're calling you, Cyril," said a woman. "You're on."

This was Cyril Crowder! But he took his time. He said, "You'll have to excuse me. I must do my stuff. Perhaps I'll see you afterward. There are drinks downstairs in the Lodge."

Cyprus sherry, Hungarian Bull's Blood that was red ink, a semisweet Spanish white, and a mongrel Corsican rosé.

* * *

The dinner I gave for Cyril Crowder, Sir Charles and Lady Barbara, Virginia Byward, and Wibbert was one of my most memorable. It was further enhanced by the appearance after dinner (I had only six chairs) of Tanya and Mr. Momma — and Mr. Momma brought his records. Naturally I left them to themselves, kept their glasses filled with some vintage Muscadet (1971), and let them become quite tipsy. Very late in the evening, Cyril took me aside. I told him again how much I had enjoyed his lecture, but he interrupted, saying, "Have you ever thought of addressing the Society?"

"I wouldn't dare."

"Oh, do."

"I'm not even a member," I said.

"We can put that right," he said, and he hollered across the room, "Charles — how about making Michael a Fellow at the next committee meeting? All in favor say, 'Aye!'"

"Aye!" came the shout from the sofa.

And Mr. Momma said, "High!"

"Motion carried," said Cyril. "Now what will you speak on?"

"First things first," I said, and uncorked a bottle of port (1972), decanted it through my hanky, and poured three inches into a schooner.

"That wine's a gentleman," said Cyril.

"So you can understand why I was so keen to lay it down."

After Sir Charles and Lady Barbara left, Mr. Momma put his records on the gramophone and did his drunken Cypriot shuffle. Wibbert waltzed with Tanya. I was tapped on the shoulder. Cyril had taken off his spectacles. He said, "May I have the pleasure?" and slipped his arm around my waist.

* * *

Friendship is algebra, but there are operations most people are too impatient or selfish to perform. Any number is possible! There is a cynical side to this. Ronald used to say that you can sleep with anyone you like — you only have to ask. That is almost entirely selfish. But one can be unselfish, even in sleeping around — in giving everything and expecting nothing but agreeable company. "Giving everything," I say; but so little is actually required — a good-natured remark, a little flattery, a drink.

But I have been bold. Not long after my election to the Royal Society I saw a production of *Streetcar Named Desire*, with Annette Frame playing Blanche Dubois. I wrote her a fan letter. She replied. I replied. We exchanged letters on a weekly basis — mine were letters, hers postcards. Then I popped the question. Would she join me for a drink? We agreed on a date and though she was leery at first she stayed until the wee hours. Now I count her as one of my dearest friends. Algebra.

I sometimes think that in my modest way I have discovered something that no one else knows. When Virginia Byward got her O.B.E. it was I who helped her choose her dress and I who drove her to the Palace. A year before I would not have believed it to be possible, and yet as we rounded Hyde Park Corner I realized we were hurrying to meet the Queen. "Alice," Virginia calls me when she is a little tipsy and tearful. But the life I have is the life I have always wanted. I am surprised that no one has realized how simple it is.

Once, I thought that in agreeing to attend my parties these

people were doing me an enormous favor, taking time off from busy schedules to flatter my vanity. Later I saw how empty their lives were. "I'd have lunch with anyone remotely human," Wibbert once said. It was the saddest thing I had ever heard. Now it is clear that if it were not for me they would drearily write their books and live drearily alone and be too proud and unimaginative to invite each other round.

They take me as I am. I pose no threat; but more, I believe I have brought some joy into their lives — as much into Mr. Momma's as Sir Charles's. It is only awkward when, very late in the evening, their gratitude gets the better of them and they insist on hearing something about my latest book. I say it's dreadful, everything's up the wall, I haven't written a word for ages. And they accept this. They even seem a bit relieved when I change the subject and uncork another bottle.

THE ENGLISH
ADVENTURE

"YOU HAVE READ already *The Times*?"

"I just did so."

"For my lateness I am deeply sorry, but there was the parking. So much of traffic in this town now. I think it is the Germans and their campings. It is fantastic."

"I hate the campings. And the Germans are a shame. You see? There are some at that table. Listen to them. Such a language."

"I much prefer the English."

"Indeed. Quite so."

"Why are you drinking *genever* at this hour?"

"For *The Times*. I had the tea and finished it. But there was still more of *The Times*. I could not have more tea, so I took some *genever*. And so I finished *The Times*, but I still have the *genever*."

"Henriet! You will be drunk for Janwillem!"

"It is easier to speak English if one is drunk, and tonight is Janwillem's church."

"A lousy night for Janwillem."

"He likes the church, Marianne. Last week he has missed the church and he has been so ashamed."

"I mean that. Happy as a louse on a dirty head. We say 'a lousy time' for a happy time."

"We say a jolly time."

"A jolly time, thank you. Did you learn this in *The Times*?"

"I learned this in England."

"Have you had a jolly time in England?"

"A lousy time."

"Henriet! You are drunk already. So I will have the tea. Last week, I had the tea, but no English. I said to the boy, 'One pot of tea and two cakes, if you please.' But he did not reply in English. It was so insulting to me. I think he did it to be wicked. When he brought the tea I said, 'Please,' but he only smiled at me. I was so deeply sorry you were not here. You would have said more."

"The young boy?".

"The old boy."

"I would have said more."

"I have been thinking last week of you in England. Proper tea, proper English. I know you already for ten years, but since we are starting this English I know you better. 'Lucky Henriet,' I have been thinking last week, 'in London with the plays and the shows, and speaking English to all the people. And I have nothing but this news and this wicked boy.' You buy that shoot in London?"

"I have bought this suit in London."

"Please. And the weather, it was nice?"

"London weather. London rain."

"It is fantastic. And the hotel, it was good?"

"We will not speak of the hotel."

"Janwillem, he enjoyed?"

"Janwillem is Janwillem. Here he is Janwillem, and in another place we go — how much money, tickets, taxis, rain, different people — he is still Janwillem. In London, at the hotel, we are in the room and I am sitting in the chair. I look out the window — a small square, with grass, very nice, and some flowers, very nice, and the wet street, so different. I turn again and I am happy until I see Janwillem is still Janwillem."

"You are not going to speak of the hotel you say!"

"I was mentioning my husband."

"He is a good man."

"Quite so, a good man. I love him. But even if he had a few faults I would love him. I would love him more and wish him to understand. The faults make the love stronger. I want him to be a bit faulty, so I can show him my love. But he is a good man. It is so hard to love a good man."

"Your English is fantastic. It is London. Last week I am here with this tea and this old boy. I am learning nothing. You are learning more English. It is London."

"It is this *genever*. And my sadness."

"We will then speak of the news. You have read already?"

"And the hotel and Janwillem. So many times I ask of him to understand this thing. 'No,' he says. 'Do not speak of it.' And he goes to his church. Even in London — the church, he is missing the church. And the children and the house. He is a good father, such a good one. But at the church, I have seen him three weeks ago, a festival, he is dancing with the other ladies, hugging them. He is so happy. Kissing them and holding hands. What is wrong with that? A man can do such things and it means nothing, but a woman cannot. No hugging — this is the fault. For a man it means nothing. He is going home in the car laughing, so happy while I am so very sad."

"I have read the front page, Henriet. And some letters. Have you seen 'appalling lack of taste'? We can discuss."

"I have seen 'appalling lack of taste' and I have seen the program on television to which it is referring."

"Fantastic."

"But I cannot discuss. I will have another *genever*. See? He knows I want it and I have not even asked. Such a pleasant boy."

"He is the boy who insulted me."

"It is only natural, Marianne. You speak in English. He is wishing to be friendly."

"I do not wish to be friendly."

"He is not the old boy. He is the young."

"I am drinking tea. He is the old."

"Perhaps he would enjoy an adventure. It means nothing to them."

"We shall speak of the news instead."

"It is the thing Janwillem does not understand at all and he will never understand. 'Do not speak of it!' But if he has an adventure I can understand. I can love him more. But he has no adventure. I have told you about Martin?"

"The librarian. He gives you books."

"He gives me pinches."

"We shall talk of the books."

"And he tells me how easy it is. It means nothing to him. He wants me to spend the night with him. I tell him impossible. An afternoon, he says. After the lunch period he puts the library in the hands of his assistant and we leave. To my house. Four hours or five. Before Janwillem comes home, before Theo breaks from school. How does he know it is so easy? But he knows too much about this. How does he know? I ask him. He has three girl friends, or two — anyway, more than one. He boasts about them, and of course I cannot have an adventure with Martin. He would boast of me."

"Maybe he would boast of you."

"Or talk about me. Men talk."

"Janwillem would be so sad."

"Janwillem would kill me. He could not stand it. I wonder if I can stand it? One day I am home with my throat — one afternoon. I am walking around the house. Strolling around the house. Not in our bedroom. Janwillem's clothes are there. He is so neat. In Theo's room. Yes, I think, that is where we would have our adventure. I go into Theo's room. Stamp collection, maps, Action-Man."

"Fantastic."

"I cannot have an adventure in my son's room with Martin. Action-Man. It would make me sad."

"I am glad I am older than you, even if my English is not good. But we will go to Croydon in April."

"In London it is wonderful even in the rain. The people are different, and so polite. If you speak to them they speak. If you don't speak they are still polite."

"*The Times* — it is very cheap in Croydon. Is it cheap in London?"

"I never read the newspaper, not once. Janwillem read it. I saw him reading it and I did not want to. I can read it here, but not there. There, I can read novels, only novels. In the hotel room, having some gin, with the rain outside, and Janwillem in his offices. No Theo, no Action-Man. There I am different, too. No headaches. I was so worried about Martin I began the migraines. Always on my day off — the migraines. And we did nothing! He only boasted and pinched, and I said, 'Yes, it is a good idea, an adventure, but not here.' "

"This talk is a bit silly and it is shaming me. Shall we discuss the news? I still have some tea left. Or books? I have seen that there is a new novel by Mister Dursday."

"Tom Thursday. Extremely violent. He shows an appalling lack of taste. I wish to speak of thumsing else."

"I have read all his books. Tom's."

"Do you remember that young American fellow — Jewish fellow — he spoke of the American novel to the Society?"

"He was fantastic."

"He asked me to meet him. That young fellow. How could I meet him? I have my family to think of, I have Janwillem. I cannot simply go off because this young Jewish fellow wishes to have an adventure. He writes me letters: 'Come! Come!' I think he is like Martin."

"Martin is not Jewish. You never said so."

"Martin and his boasting and his girl friends."

"Do not think of him, Henriet. He will give you migraines."

"Martin is gone, but I still have the migraines. I have to scream sometimes because of the migraines. Do you ever scream, Marianne?"

"I like this. This is better. Yes, one day I was making some soup. Some carrot, some potato, and chicken broth. I am looking for the, yes, the barley. The soup was in an enormous pot. The soup was boiling furiously. It was a very hot day. And then I reached for the barley. The barley was on a high shelf. I reached for it. I hit with my elbow the pot of soup and it splashed upon my arm. And then I screamed."

"I scream at Janwillem because he is so good. He mentions the church and I scream. I scream when I think of Martin, and Martin is bad."

"As you say, Martin is wicked."

"Martin is not wicked, but I cannot trust him. Always his girl friends. I would prefer to have an adventure with another man."

"I am too old for adventures, Henriet. And this is not the place."

"Those Germans — they drive twenty kilometers and have their adventures here. Look at them. You're not looking."

"I have seen Germans."

"The English people hate them as much as we do. But some do not even remember."

"How can they not remember the Germans? If once you see them you remember!"

"The young ones. They do not remember."

"Even the young ones remember!"

"In England."

"The young ones in England? I do not know the young ones in England. This tea is cold. How do you know?"

"I have asked."

"What do they say?"

"They do not know. They do not care now. It is old history."

"Where do you meet these young ones?"

"I meet them in England. In London."

"In the hotel."

"Yes, in there."

"I have not met them in Croydon."

"Do you know young ones in Croydon?"

"Henriet, everyone I meet is younger than me. So I do not notice."

"I notice. The young ones remind me."

"That they are young?"

"That I am old."

"But you are not old. What? Forty-five? Very slim and smart. Nice shoot."

"Forty-three."

"It's not old."

"If you are twenty, forty-three is old."

"This is good English conversation. Question-answer. Those Germans must think we are two English ladies, having our tea."

"I am not having tea."

"You know what I am saying."

"I did not have tea in London. In London, Janwillem has tea, he reads *The Times*, he takes his umbrella. People think he is a schoolmaster. In London, I sit by the window and read my novel and watch the rain fall. And I wait — what for? For the young to knock on my door and say, 'Madam, your adventure.'"

"You are being silly."

"In a uniform. A dark jacket and a small black tie and a tray. My adventure is on the tray. 'Just one moment,' I say. And I get up from my chair and pull the curtains so that he won't notice my age. I am very nervous, but he is more nervous, so it does not matter. I go very close to him. If you go close and he does not draw away, you know he is saying yes."

"Henriet, you have had too much to drink. Please, the news."

"I am telling you the news."

"This is not a discussion. We must discuss."

"There is nothing to discuss. I need my adventure. I have

gone to London with Janwillem for my English, but what is English if you cannot use it except to say, 'Please close the door' and 'Where is the post office?' and 'How much?' Or if you only speak it once a week at a hotel restaurant in a terrible town as this one is."

"I enjoy it. It is good enough for me. I am happy."

"I am not happy. English is not enough, Marianne. Books are very enjoyable, and lectures. But always there is Martin in the library, and that American fellow at the lectures. I ask myself: 'Am I here because of English, or do I want an adventure?'"

"What is the answer?"

"There is no answer. But English is not enough, I know that. If that could be so I could sit in the chair in the hotel and talk with the boy and be happy."

"There was a boy?"

"I have told you of the boy. With the tray and the tie. Twenty. English. Thin face. Very nervous."

"You talked with him in English?"

"Very little."

"You are smiling. No more English!"

"I can only tell you in English."

"You have said you talked very little."

"He took his clothes off, I took my clothes off. We were naked. After that, there is very little to say. 'We were naked.' It is so easy to say, 'We were naked,' if you say it in another language. It would be harder to tell Janwillem — I could say it to him in English. But he would not understand, would he? No, he would shout at me. 'Do not speak of it!' and then he would go to his church and hug and kiss those women. And formerly, I had the migraine and I have thought all those years of shooicide. Instead, I have the lessons — we have them here. But in London I know why I have the lessons. It is clear to me there. The boy. We say very little because we both can speak. So we don't need to speak. It is a small thing. As for Janwillem, it means nothing. Now we are here and it is gone, but it is not gone. There is only the English."

"A good lesson today, Henriet."

"Yes, Marianne."

"Some new words. A jolly time."

"We will say no more about my adventure."

"Next week we will read *The Times*."

"I will drink tea."

"You are fantastic."

"Yost so. That is the most faluable ting."

AFTER THE WAR

DELIA LAY IN BED and listened and studied the French in the racket. Downstairs, Mr. Rameau shouted, "Hurry up! I'm ready!" Mrs. Rameau pleaded that she had lost her handbag. The small bratty boy they called Tony kicked savagely at the wall, and Ann Marie who five times had said she could not find her good shoes had begun to cry. Mr. Rameau announced his movements: he said he was going to the door and then outside to start the car; if they weren't ready, he said, he would leave without them. He slammed the door and started the car. Mrs. Rameau shrieked. Ann Marie sobbed, "Tony called me a pig!" Someone was slapped; bureau drawers were jiggled open and then pushed. There were urgent feet on the stairs. "Wait!" The engine roared, the crying stopped. The stones in the walls of Delia's small room shook, transmitting accusations. Mrs. Rameau screamed — louder and shriller than anyone Delia had ever heard before, like a beast in a cage, a horrible and hopeless anger. Mr. Rameau, in the car, shouted a reply, but it came as if from a man raging in a stoppered bottle. There were more door slams — the sound of dropped lumber — and the ratchetings of gears, and with a loosening, lique-fying whine the car's noise trickled away. They had set out for church.

In the silence that followed, a brimming whiteness of cool vapor that soothed her ears, Delia pushed down the sheet and breathed the sunlight that blazed on her bedroom curtains. She had arrived just the night before and was to be with the Rameaus for a month, doing what her mother had called "an exchange." Later in the summer Ann Marie would join her own family in London. Arriving late at the country cottage, which was near Vence, Delia had dreaded what Ann Marie would think about a stay in London — the semi in Streatham, the outings to the Baths on the Common, the plain meals. She had brought this embarrassment to bed, but she woke up alarmed at their noise and looking forward to Ann Marie's visit, since that meant the end of her own.

The cottage, Mr. Rameau had told her proudly, had no electricity. They carried their water from a well. Their water closet (he had used this English word) was in the garden. He was, incredibly, boasting. In Paris, everything they had was modern. But this was their vacation. "We live like gypsies," he had said, "for one month of the year." And with a candle he had shown Delia to her room. He had taken the candle away, and leaving her in the darkness paused only to say that as he did not allow his daughter to use fire he could hardly be expected to let Delia do so.

The Rameaus at church, her thoughts were sweetened by sleep. She dreamed of an unfenced yellow-green field, and grass that hid her. She slept soundly in the empty house. It was not buoyancy, but the deepest submersion in sleep. She was as motionless as if she lay among the pale shells on the ocean floor.

She woke to the boom of the door downstairs swinging against the wall. Then she was summoned. She had no choice but to face them. She reached for her glasses.

* * *

"Some people," said Mr. Rameau at lunch — he was seated at the far end of the table, but she could feel the pressure of his gaze even here — "some people go out to a restaurant on Sunday. A silly superstition — they believe one should not cook food on the Lord's Day. I am modern in this way, but of course I expect you to eat what you are given, to show your appreciation. Notice how my children eat. I have told them about the war."

His lips were damp and responsive to the meat he was knifing apart, and for a moment his attention was fixed on this act. He speared a finger of meat and raised it to his mouth and spoke.

"Madame Rameau asked me whether English people ever go to church. I said I believed they did and that I was surprised when you said you would not go — "

He had a dry white face and a stiff lion-tamer's mustache. When he put his knife and fork down, and clasped his hands, his wife stopped eating and filled his plate. Madame Rameau's obedience made Delia fear this man. And Ann Marie, the friend whom she did not yet know, remained silent; her face said that she had no opinion about her father — perhaps she chose not to notice the way he held his knife in his fist. Both mother and daughter were mysteries; Delia had that morning heard them scream, but the screams did not match these silent faces. And Tony: a brat, encouraged because he was a boy, pawing his father's arm to ask a question.

Now something jarred Delia. The faces searched hers. What was it? She had been asked a question. She listened carefully to remember it.

"Yes, my parents go to church," she said. "But I don't."

"My children do as I do."

"It is my choice."

"Fifteen is rather young for choices." He said *choices* solemnly, as if speaking of a mature vice.

"Ann Marie is fifteen," said Tony, tugging the man's sleeve. "But she is bigger."

The breasts, thought Delia: Ann Marie had the beginnings of a bust — that was what the boy had meant. Delia had known she was plain, and though her eyes were green and cat-like behind her glasses — she knew this — she had not realized how plain until she had seen Ann Marie. Delia had grown eight inches in one year and her clothes, depending on when they had been bought, were either too tight or too loose. Her mother had sent her here with shorts and sandals and cotton blouses. These she was wearing now, but they seemed inappropriate to the strange meal of soup and cutlets and oily salad. The Rameaus were in the clothes they had worn to church, and Mr. Rameau, drinking wine, seemed to use the gesture of raising his glass as a way of scrutinizing her. Delia tried hard to avoid showing her shock at the food, or staring at them, but she knew what they were thinking: a dull girl, a plain girl, an English girl. She had no religion to interest them, and no small talk — she did not even like to chat in English. In French, she found it impossible to do anything but reply.

"We want you to enjoy yourself," said Mr. Rameau. "This is a primitive house, or should I say 'simple'? Paradise is simple — there is sunshine, swimming, and the food is excellent."

"Yes," said Delia, "the food is excellent." She wanted to say more — to add something to this. But she was baffled by a pleasantry she knew in advance to be insincere.

"The lettuce is fresh, from our own garden."

Why didn't Ann Marie say anything?

"Yes. It is very fresh."

Delia had ceased to be frightened by the memory of those accusatory morning noises. Now she was bored, but thoroughly bored, and it was not a neutral feeling but something like despair.

"Enough." Mr. Rameau emptied his glass of wine and waved away his wife's efforts to pour more. He said that he was going to sleep.

"I have no vacation," he said to Delia — he had been speaking to her, she realized, for the entire meal: this was her initiation. "Tomorrow I will be in town and while you are playing I will be working. This is your holiday, not mine."

In the days that followed, Delia saw that when Ann Marie was away from her father she was happier — she practiced her English and played her Rolling Stones records and they took turns giving each other new hair styles. Every morning a boy called Maurice came to the cottage and delivered to the Rameaus a loaf from his basket. Delia and Ann Marie followed him along the paths through the village and giggled when he glanced back. This was a different Ann Marie from the one at meal times and as with the mother it was Ann Marie's submissiveness that made Delia afraid of Mr. Rameau. But her pity for the girl was mingled with disbelief for the reverence the girl showed her father. Ann Marie never spoke of him.

At night, Mr. Rameau led the girls upstairs and waited in the hall with his candle until they were in bed. Then he said sharply, "Prayers!" — commanding Ann Marie, reproaching Delia — and carried his light haltingly downstairs. He held the candle in his knife grip, as if cowering from the dark.

One week, two weeks. From the first, Delia had counted the days and it was only for the briefest moments — swimming, following Maurice the breadboy, playing the records — that time passed without her sensing the weight of each second.

After breakfast Mr. Rameau always said, "I must go. No vacation for me!" And yet Delia knew, without knowing how she knew, that the man was enjoying himself — perhaps the only person in the cottage who was. One Sunday he swam. He was rough in the water, thrashing his arms, gasping, spouting water from his mouth. Pelts of hair grew on his back and, more sparsely but no less oddly, on his shoulders. He wrestled in the waves with Tony and when he had finished Madame Rameau met him at the water's edge with a dry towel. Delia had never known anyone she disliked more than this man. Her thoughts were kind toward her own father who had written twice to say how much he missed her. She could not imagine Mr. Rameau saying that to Ann Marie.

At lunch one day Tony shoved some food in his mouth and gagged. He turned aside and slowly puked on the carpet.

Delia put her fork down and shut her eyes and tasted nausea in her own throat, and when she looked up again she saw that Mr. Rameau had not moved. Damp lips, dry face: he was smiling.

"You are shocked by this little accident," he said. "But I can tell you the war was much worse than this. This is nothing. You have no idea."

Only Tony had left the room. He moaned in the parlor. And they finished their meal while Madame Rameau slopped at the vomit with a yellow rag.

* *. *

"If you behave today," said Mr. Rameau on the Friday of her third week — when had they not behaved? — "I may have a surprise for you tomorrow." He raised a long crooked finger in warning and added, "But it is not a certainty."

Delia cared so little for the man that she immediately forgot what he had said. Nor did Ann Marie mention it. Delia only remembered his promise when, after lunch on Saturday, he took an envelope from his wallet and showed four red tickets.

"For the circus," he said.

Delia looked at Ann Marie, who swallowed in appreciation. Little Tony shouted. Madame Rameau regarded Tony closely and with noticeable effort brought her floating hands together.

Delia felt a nervous thrill, the foretaste of panic from the words she had already begun to practice in her mind. She was aware she would not be asked to say them. She would have to find an opportunity.

She drew a breath and said, "Excuse me."

"A German circus," Mr. Rameau was saying. "I am told they have performed for the President, and they are at this moment in Nice. They have just come from Arabia where the entire circus was flown to perform for a sheik. They will only be in Nice for four days. We will go tomorrow. Of course, if there is any bad behavior between now and tomorrow you'll stay home."

"Excuse me," said Delia again. To steady her hand she clutched her empty glass.

Pouring Delia a glass of water, Mr. Rameau continued, "I am told there is no circus like it anywhere in the world. It is lavish in all ways. Elephants, tigers, lions — "

"I won't go to the circus," said Delia. She was at once terrified and ashamed by what she had said. She had intended to be graceful. She had been rude. For the first time this vacation her French had failed her.

Mr. Rameau was staring at her.

"I cannot go to the circus," she said.

He pushed at his mustache and said, "Well!"

Delia saw that Madame Rameau was rubbing at her mouth with her napkin, as if she wished to remove that part of her face.

Mr. Rameau had also seized his napkin. Stiff with fury he snapped the cloth at the crumbs of bread on his shirt front. "So," he said, "you intend to misbehave?"

"I don't understand." She knew each word, but they made no pattern of logic. By not going — was that misbehaving?

He faced her. "I said that if there was any bad behavior between now and tomorrow you'd stay home."

"Oh, no!" said Delia, and choked. Something pinched her throat, like a spider drawing a web through her windpipe. She gasped and drank some water. She spoke a strangled word, an old woman's croak, and tears came to her eyes from the effort of it.

At his clean portion of table, Mr. Rameau watched her struggle to begin.

"I don't go — " The words came slowly; her throat was clearing, but still the spider clung.

"Perhaps you would rather discuss this some other time?"

"I don't want to discuss it at all," she managed. "I don't go to circuses."

"There are no circuses in England?"

"Yes," she said. The word was perfect: her throat was open. "There are circuses in England. But I haven't gone since I was very young."

Mr. Rameau said to his wife, "She has not gone since she was very young." And to Delia, "Have you a reason?"

"I don't enjoy circuses."

"Ah, but you said that you once went! When you were young." He smiled, believing he had trapped her. "You enjoyed them then?"

"But I was very young," she said, insisting on the importance of the word he had mocked. "I did not know anything about them."

"The English," said Mr. Rameau, and again he turned to his wife. "Such seriousness of purpose, such dedication. What is there to know about a circus? It exists purely for enjoyment — there is nothing to understand. It is laughter and animals, a little exotic and out of the ordinary. You see how she makes it a problem?"

Mrs. Rameau, who had mistaken Delia's gasping for terror, said, "She does not want to go. Why don't we leave it at that?"

"Why? Because she has not given a reason."

The words she had practiced formed in her mind, her whole coherent reason. But it was phrased too pompously for something so simple, and as the man would have no reply for it she knew it would give offense. But she was glad for this chance to challenge him and only wished that her French was better, for each time he replied he seemed to correct by repeating it the pronunciation of what she said.

"I don't believe she has a reason, unless being English is the reason. Being English is the reason for so much."

"Being French" — she was safe merely repeating what he

had said: his manner had shown her the rules — "being French is the reason for so much."

"We enjoy circuses. This is a great circus. They have performed for kings and presidents. You might say we are childish, but" — he passed a finger across his mustache — "what of those kings?" He spoke to his wife. "What of those kings, eh?"

Ann Marie took a deep breath, but she said nothing. Tony made pellets of bread. Madame Rameau, Delia could see, wanted her husband to stop this.

Delia said, "The animals do tricks. People think they are clever tricks. A tiger jumps through a hoop. An elephant dances. The dogs walk on their back legs — "

"We are familiar with the tricks," said Mr. Rameau testily. "We have been to circuses."

"The circus people are cruel to the animals."

"This is totally untrue!" His hands flew up and Delia thought for a moment that he was about to slap her face.

The violence in his motioning hands spurred her on. "They are cruel to them in the way they teach the animals to do tricks."

"She knows so much for someone who never goes to circuses," said Mr. Rameau, and brought his hands down to the table.

"They use electric shocks. They starve them. They beat them." She looked up. Mr. Rameau showed no emotion, and now his hands were beneath the table. "They bind their legs with wire. They inflict pain on the animals. The animals are so hurt and afraid they do these tricks. They seem clever, but it is fear. They obey because they are afraid."

Delia thought this would move him, but he had begun again to smile.

"You are fifteen. You were born in nineteen sixty-two, the same year as Ann Marie."

"Yes."

"So you don't know."

"I have been told this about the circus by people who do know."

"Now I am not speaking about the circus. I am speaking about the war. You are very concerned about the animals — "

She hated this man's face.

" — but have you any idea what the Germans did to us in the war? Perhaps you are right — the animals are mistreated from time to time. But they are not killed. Surely it is worse to be killed or tortured?"

"Some animals are tortured. It is what I said."

But he was still speaking. "Of course, one hears how bad it was for the Jews, but listen — I was your age in nineteen forty-two. I remember the Germans. The Jews tell one story — everyone knows this story. Yes, perhaps it was as bad for them as they say. I don't speak for other people — I speak for myself. And I can tell you that we starved. We were beaten. Our legs were tied. And sometimes for days we were left in the dark of our houses, never knowing whether we would live to see the light. It made some people do things they would not normally do, but I learned to respect my parents. I understood how terrible it must have been for them. I obeyed them. They knew more than I did and later I realized how dreadful it was. It was not a circus. It was war."

He made it an oration, using his hands to help his phrases through the air, and yet Delia felt that for all the anonymity of his blustering he was expressing private thoughts and a particular pain.

Madame Rameau said, "Please be calm, Jean. You are being very hard on the girl."

"I am giving this young girl the benefit of my experience."

Still the woman seemed ashamed, and she winced when he began again.

"I have seen people grovel to German army officers, simply to get a crust of bread. It did not horrify me. It taught me respect, and respect is something you do not know a great deal about, from what you have said. The Jews tell another story, but remember — it was very bad for us. After the war, many people forgot, but I suffered, so I do not forget."

"It might be better if we did not go to the circus," said Madame Rameau.

"I don't want to go to the circus," said Ann Marie.

Tony had already begun to protest. "I do! I am going!"

"Yes," said Mr. Rameau and struck his son affectionately on the shoulder. "We will all go to the circus. The tickets are paid for."

Delia had resolved to say nothing more.

Madame Rameau said, "The girl does not have to go, if she would rather stay home with me."

"If she wishes to stay at home she may stay. So we have an extra ticket. You will come to the circus with us, my dear."

"I am not sure I want to go."

"You will go," he said promptly. "We will all go. It is what our English guest insists upon."

Madame Rameau reached for Delia but stopped short of touching her. She said, "I will leave some soup for you. And a cutlet."

"No need for the cutlet," said Mr. Rameau. "She never eats much of what we give her. She will only leave it on her plate."

"You won't be afraid to be here alone?" Madame Rameau was close to tears.

Mr. Rameau answered for Delia. "It is the animals who are afraid! You heard what she said. She will not be afraid while we are away. She might be very happy."

* * *

His white face was a hard dull slab when in the flower-scented twilight, and just before taking his family away to the circus, he stood in the doorway and said, "No matches. No candles. My advice to you is to eat now while there is some light, and

then go to bed. We will not be late. Eight o'clock, nine
o'clock. And tomorrow we will tell you what you missed."

He sounded almost kindly, his warning a gentle consolation.
He ended softly, but just as she thought he was going to lean
forward to touch her or kiss her he abruptly turned away,
making Delia flinch. He drove the car fast to the road.

Delia ate in the mottled half-dark of the back kitchen. She
had no appetite in the dim room, and the dimness which rapidly soaked into night made her alert. The church bell in the
village signaled eight; the Rameaus did not come back. At nine
she grew restive. It was less dark outside with stars and the
moon in ragged clouds like a watch crystal. The windows
were open, the sound of distant cars moved through the
hedges, the trees in the garden — it was a trick of the dark —
rattled dry leaves in her room.

She wondered if she were afraid. She started to sing and
frightened herself with her clear off-key cry. She toyed with
the thought of running away, leaving a vague note behind for
Mr. Rameau — and she laughed at the thought of his panic:
the phone calls, the police, his helplessness. But she was not
young enough or old enough to run. She was satisfied with
the stand she had taken against him, but what sustained her was
her hatred for him. It was not the circus anymore, not those
poor animals, but the man himself who was in his wickedness
more important than the animals' suffering. She had not given
in. He was the enemy and he was punishing her for challenging him. Those last coy words of his were meant to punish her.
She went to the doorway to hear the church bell better.

At midnight she anxiously counted and she was afraid —
that their car had been wrecked and the whole family killed;
afraid of her hatred for him that had made her forget the circus. It was too late to remain in the doorway, and when Delia
withdrew into the house she knew by the darkness and the
time how he had calculated his punishment. She saw that his
punishment was his own fear. The coward he was would be

afraid of the thickened dark of this room. It took her fear away.

So she did not hear the car. She heard their feet on the path, some whispers, the scrape of the heavy door. He was in front; Madame Rameau hurried past him, struck a match to a candle and held the flame up. He was carrying his son.

"Still awake?" he said. His exaggerated kindness was mockery. "Look, she is waiting for us."

The candle flame trembled in the woman's trembling hand. "You'll go next time, won't you?"

Delia was smiling. She wanted him to come close enough in that poor light to see her smile.

He repeated his question, demanding a reply, but he was so loud the child woke and cried out of pure terror, and without warning arched his back in instinctive struggle and tried to get free of the hard arms which held him.

WORDS ARE DEEDS

ON ENTERING the restaurant in Corte, Professor Sheldrick saw the woman standing near the bar. He decided then that he would take her away with him, perhaps marry her. When she offered him a menu and he realized she was a waitress he was more certain she would accompany him that very day to the hotel, where he had a reservation, on the coast at Ile-Rousse. Not even the suspicion that it was her husband behind the counter — he had a drooping black mustache and was older than she — deterred him as he planned his moves. The man looked like a brute, in any case; and Sheldrick was prepared to offer that woman everything he had.

His wife had left him in Marseilles. She said she wanted to live her own life. She was almost forty and she explained that if she waited any longer no man would look twice at her. She refused to argue or be drawn; her mind was made up. It was Sheldrick who did all the imploring, but it did no good.

He said, "What did I do?"

"It's what you said."

Words are deeds: he knew that was what she meant. And not one but an accumulation of them over a dozen years. The marriage, he knew, had been ruined long before. He was content to live in those ruins and he had believed she needed him. But there in Marseilles she declared she was leaving him. The words she said with such simple directness weakened him; he ached as if in speaking to him that way she had trampled him. He agreed to let her have the house and a certain amount of money every month.

He said, "I'll suffer."

"You deserve to suffer."

Her manner was girlish and hopeful, his almost elderly. She went home; but when it was time for him to return home he could see no point to it, nor any reason to work. He was a professor of French literature at a college in Connecticut: the semester was starting. But from the day his wife left him, Sheldrick answered no letters and made no plans and did not think about the future. What was the point? He did nothing, because nothing mattered. He had set out on this trip feeling lucky, if a bit burdened by his wife. Now the summer was over, his wife had left him, and he began to believe that she had taken the world with her.

He no longer recognized the importance of anything he had ever done before, but his feeling of failure was so complete he felt he did not exist except as a polite and harmless creature who, all his defenses removed, faced extinction. His wife had pushed their boulder aside and left him exposed, like a soft blind worm.

In this mood, one of uselessness, he felt entirely without obligation. The world was illusion — he had invented a marriage and an existence, and it had all vanished. He was a victim twitching in air, with a small voice. What he had mistaken for concreteness was vapor. Only lovers had faith. But he didn't want his wife back; he wanted nothing.

His surprise was that he could enter a strange restaurant in a remote Corsican town and see a woman and want to marry her. He wondered if defeat had made him bold. This island, the first landscape he had seen as a newly single man, had a wild shipwrecked look to it that suited his recklessness. He would ask that woman to leave with him.

He was bewitched by her peculiar beauty, which was the

beauty of certain trees he had been admiring all afternoon in the drive from the stinks of Cateraggio. She was slim, like those trees, and unlike any woman he had seen on this island. He knew then that he would not leave Corte without her. She was the embodiment of everything he loved in Corsica. The idea that he would take her with him was definite. There was no doubt in his mind; it was rash and necessary. And while he found a seat and ordered a drink and then chose at random from the menu, he had already decided on his course of action. It only remained for him to begin.

His French was fluent. Indeed, he affected a slight French accent, a stutter in his throat and the trace of a lisp, when he spoke English. But language was the least of it. She had small shoulders and almost no breasts, and slender legs, and her hair was cut short. He spoke to her about the food, but only to detain her, so he could be near her. She smelled of lilies. She brought the wine; his meal; the dessert — fruit; coffee, which her husband — almost certainly her husband — made on the machine. And each time, he said something more, trying to grow intimate, to make her see him. He had no clear plan. He would not leave the town without her. He was due in Ile-Rousse that night. She wore a finely spun sweater. She was not dressed for a restaurant: she was no waitress. Her husband owned the place — he forced her to help him run it. Sheldrick guessed at these things and by degrees he began to understand that though he had only happened upon her, she was waiting for him.

She approached him with the bill folded on a saucer. He invited her to look at it, and when she bent close to him, peering at the bill, he said, "Please — come with me."

He feared she might be startled: for seconds he knew he had said something dangerous. But she was looking at the bill. Was this pretense? Was she stalling?

He said, "I have a car."

She was expressionless. She touched the bill with a sharp red claw.

Trying to control his voice, Sheldrick said, "I love you and I want you to come with me."

She faced him, turning her green eyes on him, and he knew she was scrutinizing him, wondering if he were crazy. He smiled helplessly, and her gaze seemed to soften, a pale glitter pricking the green.

His hands trembled as he placed his money on the saucer.

She said, "I will bring you your change."

The she was gone. Sheldrick forced himself to stare at the tablecloth, so as not to betray his passion to the man he supposed was her husband.

She did not return immediately. Was she telling her husband what he had said? He could hardly blame her. What he had asked her in a pleading whisper was so insane an impulse that he knew he must have frightened her. And yet he did not regret it. He knew he had had to say it or he would not have forgiven himself and would have suffered for the rest of his life. After five minutes he assumed she had gone to the police; he imagined that now many people knew the mad request he had made to this woman.

In the same stately way that she had approached before, she crossed the restaurant with the saucer, and with some formality, bowing slightly as she did so, placed it before him. She went away, back to the bar where he had first seen her.

There was nothing more. She had not replied; she had not said a word. So, without a word, there was no blame; and it had all passed, like a spell of fever. Now it could remain a secret. She had been kind enough to let him go without making a jackass of himself.

He plucked at his change, keenly aware of the charade he was performing in leaving her a tip. But gathering the coins, he saw the folded bill at the bottom of the saucer, and the sentence written on it. The scribbled words made him breathless and stupid, the fresh ink made him flush like an illiterate. He labored to read it, but it was simple. It said: *I will be at the statue of Paoli after we close.*

He put the bill into his pocket and left her ten francs, and not looking at her again he hurried out of the restaurant. He walked, turning corners, on rising streets that became steps, and climbed a stone staircase on the ramparts that towered over Corte. Alone here, he read the sentence again and was joyful on these ruined battlements and thrilled by the wind in the flag above him. Beneath him in the rocky valleys and on hillsides were the trees he had come to love.

He gave her an hour. At five, in brilliant twilight, he found his car, which was parked near the restaurant. The steel shutters of the restaurant were across the windows and padlocked. It was Sunday; the cobblestone streets of this hilltop town were deserted, and he could imagine that he was the only person alive in Corte. Not wishing to be conspicuous, he decided that it was better to drive slowly through the Place Paoli than to walk.

He found it easily, an irregular plaza of sloping cobbles, and rounding the statue he saw her, wearing a short jacket, carrying a handbag, her white face fixed on him. He stopped. Before he could speak she was beside him in the car.

"Quickly," she said. "Don't stop."

Her decisiveness stunned him, his feet and hands were numb, he was slow.

"Do you hear me?" she said. "Drive — drive!"

He remembered how to drive, and skidded out of the town, making it topple in his rearview mirror. She looked back; she was afraid, then excited, her face shining. She looked at him with curiosity and said, "Where are we going?"

"Ile-Rousse," he said. "I have a room at the Hotel Bonaparte."

"And after that?"

"I don't know. Maybe Porto."

"Porto is disgusting."

This disconcerted him: his wife had often spoken of Porto. One of her regrets when she left him, perhaps her only regret

— though she had not put it this way — was that they would not be able to visit Porto, as they had planned.

The woman said, "It is all Germans and Americans."

"I am an American."

"But the other kind."

"We're all the same."

She said, "I would like to visit America."

"I hope I never see the place again as long as I live," he said.

She stared at Sheldrick but said nothing.

"You are very beautiful."

"Thank you. You are kind."

"Beautiful," he said, "like Corsica."

She said, "I hate Corsica. These people are savages."

"You're not a savage."

"I am not a Corsican," she said. "My husband is one." She glanced through the rear window. "But that is finished now."

It had all happened quickly, the courtship back in the restaurant, and she had greeted him at the statue like an old busy friend ("Do you hear me?"). This was something else, another phase; so he dared the question. "Why did you come with me?"

She said, "I wanted to. I have been planning to leave for a year. But something always goes wrong. You worried me a little. I thought you were a policeman — why do you drive so slow?"

"I'm not used to these roads."

"André — my husband — he drives like a maniac."

Sheldrick said, "I'm a university professor," and at once hated himself for saying it.

The road was tortuous. He could not imagine anyone going fast on these curves, but the woman (what was her name? when could he ask her?) repeated that her husband raced his car here. Sheldrick was aware of how the car was toiling in second gear, of his damp palms slipping on the steering wheel. He said, "If you're not Corsican, what are you?"

"I am French," she said. Then, "When André sees that I have left him, he will try to kill me. All Corsicans are like that — bloodthirsty. And jealous. He will want to kill you, too."

Sheldrick said, "Funny. I hadn't thought of that."

She said, "They all have guns. André hunts wild boar in the mountains. Those mountains. He's a wonderful shot. Those were our only happy times — hunting, in the first years."

"I hate guns," said Sheldrick.

"All Americans like guns."

"Not this American," he said. She sighed in a deliberate, almost actressy way. He was trying, but already he could see she disliked him a little — and with no reason. He had rescued her! On a straight road he would have leaned back and sped to the hotel in silence. But these hills, and the slowness of the car, made him impatient. He could think of nothing to say; and she was no help. She sat silently in her velvet jacket.

Finally, he said, "Do you have any children?"

"What do you take me for?" she said. Her shriek jarred him. "Do you think if I had children I would just abandon them like a slut in the afternoon and go off with a complete stranger? Do you?"

"I'm sorry."

"You're not sorry," she said. "You did take me for a slut."

He began again to apologize.

"Drive," she said, interrupting him. She was staring at him again. "Your suit," she said. "Surely, it is rather shabby even for a university professor?"

"I hadn't noticed," he said coldly.

She said, "I hate your tie."

WHITE LIES

NORMALLY, in describing the life cycle of ectoparasites for my notebook, I went into great detail, since I hoped to publish an article about the strangest ones when I returned home from Africa. The one exception was *Dermatobia bendiense*. I could not give it my name; I was not its victim. And the description? One word: *Jerry*. I needed nothing more to remind me of the discovery, and though I fully intend to test my findings in the pages of an entomological journal, the memory is still too horrifying for me to reduce it to science.

Jerry Benda and I shared a house on the compound of a bush school. Every Friday and Saturday night he met an African girl named Ameena at the Rainbow Bar and brought her home in a taxi. There was no scandal: no one knew. In the morning, after breakfast, Ameena did Jerry's ironing (I did my own) and the black cook carried her back to town on the crossbar of his old bike. That was a hilarious sight. Returning from my own particular passion, which was collecting insects in the fields near our house, I often met them on the road: Jika in his cook's khakis and skullcap pedaling the long-legged Ameena — I must say, she reminded me of a highly desirable insect. They yelped as they clattered down the road, the deep ruts making the bicycle bell hiccup like an alarm clock.

A stranger would have assumed these Africans were man and wife, making an early morning foray to the market. The local people paid no attention.

Only I knew that these were the cook and mistress of a young American who was regarded at the school as very charming in his manner and serious in his work. The cook's laughter was a nervous giggle — he was afraid of Ameena. But he was devoted to Jerry and far too loyal to refuse to do what Jerry asked of him.

Jerry was deceitful, but at the time I did not think he was imaginative enough to do any damage. And yet his was not the conventional double life that most white people led in Africa. Jerry had certain ambitions: ambition makes more liars than egotism does. But Jerry was so careful, his lies such modest calculations, he was always believed. He said he was from Boston. "Belmont actually," he told me, when I said I was from Medford. His passport — *Bearer's address* — said Watertown. He felt he had to conceal it. That explained a lot: the insecurity of living on the lower slopes of the long hill, between the smoldering steeples of Boston and the clean, high-priced air of Belmont. We are probably no more class conscious than the British, but when we make class an issue it seems more than snobbery. It becomes a bizarre spectacle, a kind of attention seeking, and I cannot hear an American speaking of his social position without thinking of a human fly, one of those tiny men in grubby capes whom one sometimes sees clinging to the brickwork of a tall building.

What had begun as fantasy had, after six months of his repeating it in our insignificant place, made it seem like fact. Jerry didn't know Africa: his one girl friend stood for the whole continent. And of course he lied to her. I had the impression that it was one of the reasons Jerry wanted to stay in Africa. If you tell enough lies about yourself, they take hold. It becomes impossible ever to go back, since that means facing the truth. In Africa, no one could dispute what Jerry said he was: a wealthy Bostonian, from a family of some distinction, adventuring in Third World philanthropy before inheriting his father's business.

Rereading the above, I think I may be misrepresenting him. Although he was undeniably a fraud in some ways, his fraudulence was the last thing you noticed about him. What you saw first was a tall good-natured person in his early twenties, confidently casual, with easy charm and a gift for ingenious flattery. When I told him I had majored in entomology he called me "Doctor." This later became "Doc." He showed exaggerated respect to the gardeners and washerwomen at the school, using the politest phrases when he spoke to them. He always said "sir" to the students ("You, sir, are a lazy little creep"), which baffled them and won them over. The cook adored him, and even the cook's cook — who was lame and fourteen and ragged — liked Jerry to the point where the poor boy would go through the compound stealing flowers from the Inkpens' garden to decorate our table. While I was merely tolerated as an unattractive and near-sighted bug collector, Jerry was courted by the British wives in the compound. The wife of the new headmaster, Lady Alice (Sir Godfrey Inkpen had been knighted for his work in the Civil Service) usually stopped in to see Jerry when her husband was away. Jerry was gracious with her and anxious to make a good impression. Privately, he said, "She's all tits and teeth."

"Why is it," he said to me one day, "that the white women have all the money and the black ones have all the looks?"

"I didn't realize you were interested in money."

"Not for itself, Doc," he said. "I'm interested in what it can buy."

*   *   *

No matter how hard I tried, I could not get used to hearing Ameena's squawks of pleasure from the next room, or Jerry's elbows banging against the wall. At any moment, I expected their humpings and slappings to bring down the boxes of mounted butterflies I had hung there. At breakfast, Jerry was his urbane self, sitting at the head of the table while Ameena cackled.

He held a teapot in each hand. "What will it be, my dear? Chinese or Indian tea? Marmalade or jam? Poached or scrambled? And may I suggest a kipper?"

"*Wopusa!*" Ameena would say. "Idiot!"

She was lean, angular, and wore a scarf in a handsome turban on her head. "I'd marry that girl tomorrow," Jerry said, "if she had fifty grand." Her breasts were full and her skin was like velvet; she looked majestic, even doing the ironing. And when I saw her ironing, it struck me how Jerry inspired devotion in people.

But not any from me. I think I resented him most because he was new. I had been in Africa for two years and had replaced any ideas of sexual conquest with the possibility of a great entomological discovery. But he was not interested in my experience. There was a great deal I could have told him. In the meantime, I watched Jika taking Ameena into town on his bicycle, and I added specimens to my collection.

* * *

Then, one day, the Inkpens' daughter arrived from Rhodesia to spend her school holidays with her parents.

We had seen her the day after she arrived, admiring the roses in her mother's garden, which adjoined ours. She was about seventeen, and breathless and damp; and so small I at once imagined this pink butterfly struggling in my net. Her name was Petra (her parents called her "Pet"), and her pretty bloom was recklessness and innocence. Jerry said, "I'm going to marry her."

"I've been thinking about it," he said the next day. "If I just invite her I'll look like a wolf. If I invite the three of them it'll seem as if I'm stage-managing it. So I'll invite the parents

— for some inconvenient time — and they'll have no choice but to ask me if they can bring the daughter along, too. *They'll* ask *me* if they can bring her. Good thinking? It'll have to be after dark — they'll be afraid of someone raping her. Sunday's always family day, so how about Sunday at seven? High tea. They will deliver her into my hands."

The invitation was accepted. And Sir Godfrey said, "I hope you don't mind if we bring our daughter — "

More than anything, I wished to see whether Jerry would bring Ameena home that Saturday night. He did — I suppose he did not want to arouse Ameena's suspicions — and on Sunday morning it was breakfast as usual and "What will it be, my dear?"

But everything was not as usual. In the kitchen, Jika was making a cake and scones. The powerful fragrance of baking, so early on a Sunday morning, made Ameena curious. She sniffed and smiled and picked up her cup. Then she asked: What was the cook making?

"Cakes," said Jerry. He smiled back at her.

Jika entered timidly with some toast.

"You're a better cook than I am," Ameena said in Chinyanja. "I don't know how to make cakes."

Jika looked terribly worried. He glanced at Jerry.

"Have a cake," said Jerry to Ameena.

Ameena tipped the cup to her lips and said slyly, "Africans don't eat cakes for breakfast."

"*We* do," said Jerry, with guilty rapidity. "It's an old American custom."

Ameena was staring at Jika. When she stood up he winced. Ameena said, "I have to make water." It was one of the few English sentences she knew.

Jerry said, "I think she suspects something."

As I started to leave with my net and my chloroform bottle I heard a great fuss in the kitchen, Jerry telling Ameena not to do the ironing, Ameena protesting, Jika groaning. But Jerry was angry, and soon the bicycle was bumping away from the house: Jika pedaling, Ameena on the crossbar.

"She just wanted to hang around," said Jerry. "Guess what the bitch was doing? She was ironing a drip-dry shirt!"

*　　*　　*

It was early evening when the Inkpens arrived, but night fell before tea was poured. Petra sat between her proud parents, saying what a super house we had, what a super school it was, how super it was to have a holiday here. Her monotonous ignorance made her even more desirable.

Perhaps for our benefit — to show her off — Sir Godfrey asked her leading questions. "Mother tells me you've taken up knitting" and "Mother says you've become quite a whiz at math." Now he said, "I hear you've been doing some riding."

"Heaps, actually," said Petra. Her face was shining. "There are some stables near the school."

Dances, exams, picnics, house parties: Petra gushed about her Rhodesian school. And in doing so she made it seem a distant place — not an African country at all, but a special preserve of superior English recreations.

"That's funny," I said. "Aren't there Africans there?"

Jerry looked sharply at me.

"Not at the school," said Petra. "There are some in town. The girls call them nig-nogs." She smiled. "But they're quite sweet actually."

"The Africans, dear?" asked Lady Alice.

"The girls," said Petra.

Her father frowned.

Jerry said, "What do you think of this place?"

"Honestly, I think it's super."

"Too bad it's so dark at the moment," said Jerry. "I'd like to show you my frangipani."

"Jerry's famous for that frangipani," said Lady Alice.

Jerry had gone to the French windows to indicate the general direction of the bush. He gestured toward the darkness and said, "It's somewhere over there."

"I see it," said Petra.

The white flowers and the twisted limbs of the frangipani were clearly visible in the headlights of an approaching car.

Sir Godfrey said, "I think you have a visitor."

The Inkpens were staring at the taxi. I watched Jerry. He had turned pale, but kept his composure. "Ah, yes," he said, "it's the sister of one of our pupils." He stepped outside to intercept her, but Ameena was too quick for him. She hurried past him, into the parlor where the Inkpens sat dumbfounded. Then Sir Godfrey, who had been surprised into silence, stood up and offered Ameena his chair.

Ameena gave a nervous grunt and faced Jerry. She wore the black satin cloak and sandals of a village Muslim. I had never seen her in anything but a tight dress and high heels; in that long cloak she looked like a very dangerous fly which had buzzed into the room on stiff wings.

"How nice to see you," said Jerry. Every word was right, but his voice had become shrill. "I'd like you to meet — "

Ameena flapped the wings of her cloak in embarrassment and said, "I cannot stay. And I am sorry for this visit." She spoke in her own language. Her voice was calm and even apologetic.

"Perhaps she'd like to sit down," said Sir Godfrey, who was still standing.

"I think she's fine," said Jerry, backing away slightly.

Now I saw the look of horror on Petra's face. She glanced up and down, from the dark shawled head to the cracked feet, then gaped in bewilderment and fear.

At the kitchen door, Jika stood with his hands over his ears.

"Let's go outside," said Jerry in Chinyanja.

"It is not necessary," said Ameena. "I have something for you. I can give it to you here."

Jika ducked into the kitchen and shut the door.

"Here," said Ameena. She fumbled with her cloak.

Jerry said quickly, "No," and turned as if to avert the thrust of a dagger.

But Ameena had taken a soft gift-wrapped parcel from the folds of her cloak. She handed it to Jerry and, without turning to us, flapped out of the room. She became invisible as soon as she stepped into the darkness. Before anyone could speak, the taxi was speeding away from the house.

Lady Alice said, "How very odd."

"Just a courtesy call," said Jerry, and amazed me with a succession of plausible lies. "Her brother's in Form Four — a very bright boy, as a matter of fact. She was rather pleased by how well he'd done in his exams. She stopped in to say thanks."

"That's *very* African," said Sir Godfrey.

"It's lovely when people drop in," said Petra. "It's really quite a compliment."

Jerry was smiling weakly and eyeing the window, as if he expected Ameena to thunder in once again and split his head open. Or perhaps not. Perhaps he was congratulating himself that it had all gone so smoothly.

Lady Alice said, "Well, aren't you going to open it?"

"Open what?" said Jerry, and then he realized that he was holding the parcel. "You mean this?"

"I wonder what it could be," said Petra.

I prayed that it was nothing frightening. I had heard stories of jilted lovers sending aborted fetuses to the men who had wronged them.

"I adore opening parcels," said Petra.

Jerry tore off the wrapping paper, but satisfied himself that it was nothing incriminating before he showed it to the Inkpens.

"Is it a shirt?" said Lady Alice.

"It's a beauty," said Sir Godfrey.

It was red and yellow and green, with embroidery at the collar and cuffs; an African design. Jerry said, "I should give it back. It's a sort of bribe, isn't it?"

"Absolutely not," said Sir Godfrey. "I insist you keep it."

"Put it on!" said Petra.

Jerry shook his head. Lady Alice said, "Oh, do!"

"Some other time," said Jerry. He tossed the shirt aside and told a long humorous story of his sister's wedding reception on the family yacht. And before the Inkpens left he asked Sir Godfrey with old-fashioned formality if he might be allowed to take Petra on a day trip to the local tea estate.

"You're welcome to use my car if you like," said Sir Godfrey.

*　　*　　*

It was only after the Inkpens had gone that Jerry began to tremble. He tottered to a chair, lit a cigarette, and said, "That was the worst hour of my life. Did you see her? Jesus! I thought that was the end. But what did I tell you? She suspected something!"

"Not necessarily," I said.

He kicked the shirt — I noticed he was hesitant to touch it — and said, "What's this all about then?"

"As you told Inky — it's a present."

"She's a witch," said Jerry. "She's up to something."

"You're crazy," I said. "What's more, you're unfair. You kicked her out of the house. She came back to ingratiate herself by giving you a present — a new shirt for all the ones she didn't have a chance to iron. But she saw our neighbors. I don't think she'll be back."

"What amazes me," said Jerry, "is your presumption. I've been sleeping with Ameena for six months, while you've been playing with yourself. And here you are trying to tell me about her! You're incredible."

Jerry had the worst weakness of the liar: he never believed anything you told him.

I said, "What are you going to do with the shirt?"

Clearly this had been worrying him. But he said nothing.

Late that night, working with my specimens, I smelled acrid

smoke. I went to the window. The incinerator was alight; Jika was coughing and stirring the flames with a stick.

* * *

The next Saturday, Jerry took Petra to the tea estate in Sir Godfrey's gray Humber. I spent the day with my net, rather resenting the thought that Jerry had all the luck. First Ameena, now Petra. And he had ditched Ameena. There seemed no end to his arrogance or — what was more annoying — his luck. He came back to the house alone. I vowed that I would not give him a chance to do any sexual boasting. I stayed in my room, but less than ten minutes after he arrived home he was knocking on my door.

"I'm busy," I yelled.

"Doc, this is serious."

He entered rather breathless, fever-white and apologetic. This was not someone who had just made a sexual conquest — I knew as soon as I saw him that it had all gone wrong. So I said, "How does she bump?"

He shook his head. He looked very pale. He said, "I couldn't."

"So she turned you down." I could not hide my satisfaction.

"She was screaming for it," he said, rather primly. "She's seventeen, Doc. She's locked in a girls' school half the year. She even found a convenient haystack. But I had to say no. In fact, I couldn't get away from her fast enough."

"Something *is* wrong," I said. "Do you feel all right?"

He ignored the question. "Doc," he said, "remember when Ameena barged in. Just think hard. Did she touch me? Listen, this is important."

I told him I could not honestly remember whether she had touched him. The incident was so pathetic and embarrassing I had tried to blot it out.

"I knew something like this was going to happen. But I don't understand it." He was talking quickly and unbuttoning his shirt. Then he took it off. "Look at this. Have you ever seen anything like it?"

At first I thought his body was covered by welts. But what I had taken to be welts were a mass of tiny reddened patches, like fly bites, some already swollen into bumps. Most of them — and by far the worst — were on his back and shoulders. They were as ugly as acne and had given his skin that same shine of infection.

"It's interesting," I said.

"Interesting!" he screamed. "It looks like syphilis and all you can say is it's interesting. Thanks a lot."

"Does it hurt?"

"Not too much," he said. "I noticed it this morning before I went out. But I think they've gotten worse. That's why nothing happened with Petra. I was too scared to take my shirt off."

"I'm sure she wouldn't have minded if you'd kept it on."

"I couldn't risk it," he said. "What if it's contagious?"

He put calamine lotion on it and covered it carefully with gauze, and the next day it was worse. Each small bite had swelled to a pimple, and some of them seemed on the point of erupting: a mass of small warty boils. That was on Sunday. On Monday I told Sir Godfrey that Jerry had a bad cold and could not teach. When I got back to the house that afternoon, Jerry said that it was so painful he couldn't lie down. He had spent the afternoon sitting bolt upright in a chair.

"It was that shirt," he said. "Ameena's shirt. She did something to it."

I said, "You're lying. Jika burned that shirt — remember?"

"She touched me," he said. "Doc, maybe it's not a curse — I'm not superstitious anyway. Maybe she gave me syph."

"Let's hope so."

"What do you mean by that!"

"I mean, there's a cure for syphilis."

"Suppose it's not that?"

"We're in Africa," I said.

This terrified him, as I knew it would.

He said, "Look at my back and tell me if it looks as bad as it feels."

He crouched under the lamp. His back was grotesquely inflamed. The eruptions had become like nipples, much bigger and with a bruised discoloration. I pressed one. He cried out. Watery liquid leaked from a pustule.

"That hurt!" he said.

"Wait." I saw more infection inside the burst boil — a white clotted mass. I told him to grit his teeth. "I'm going to squeeze this one."

I pressed it between my thumbs and as I did a small white knob protruded. It was not pus — not liquid. I kept on pressing and Jerry yelled with shrill ferocity until I was done. Then I showed him what I had squeezed from his back; it was on the tip of my tweezers — a live maggot.

"It's a worm!"

"A larva."

"You know about these things. You've seen this before, haven't you?"

I told him the truth. I had never seen one like it before in my life. It was not in any textbook I had ever seen. And I told him more: there were, I said, perhaps two hundred of them, just like the one wriggling on my tweezers, in those boils on his body.

Jerry began to cry.

*   *   *

That night I heard him writhing in his bed, and groaning, and if I had not known better I would have thought Ameena was with him. He turned and jerked and thumped like a lover maddened by desire; and he whimpered, too, seeming to savor the kind of pain that is indistinguishable from sexual pleasure. But it was no more passion than the movement of those maggots in his flesh. In the morning, gray with sleeplessness, he said he felt like a corpse. Truly, he looked as if he was being eaten alive.

An illness you read about is never as bad as the real thing. Boy Scouts are told to suck the poison out of snakebites. But a snakebite — swollen and black and running like a leper's sore — is so horrible I can't imagine anyone capable of staring at it, much less putting his mouth on it. It was that way with Jerry's boils. All the textbooks on earth could not have prepared me for their ugliness, and what made them even more repellent was the fact that his face and hands were free of them. He was infected from his neck to his waist, and down his arms; his face was haggard, and in marked contrast to his sores.

I said, "We'll have to get you to a doctor."

"A witch doctor."

"You're serious!"

He gasped and said, "I'm dying, Doc. You have to help me."

"We can borrow Sir Godfrey's car. We could be in Blantyre by midnight."

Jerry said, "I can't last until midnight."

"Take it easy," I said. "I have to go over to the school. I'll say you're still sick. I don't have any classes this afternoon, so when I get back I'll see if I can do anything for you."

"There are witch doctors around here," he said. "You can find one — they know what to do. It's a curse."

I watched his expression change as I said, "Maybe it's the curse of the white worm." He deserved to suffer, after what he had done, but his face was so twisted in fear, I added, "There's only one thing to do. Get those maggots out. It might work."

"Why did I come to this fucking place!"

But he shut his eyes and was silent: he knew why he had left home.

When I returned from the school ("And how is our ailing

friend?" Sir Godfrey had asked at morning assembly), the house seemed empty. I had a moment of panic, thinking that Jerry — unable to stand the pain — had taken an overdose. I ran into the bedroom. He lay asleep on his side, but woke when I shook him.

"Where's Jika?" I said.

"I gave him the week off," said Jerry. "I didn't want him to see me. What are you doing?"

I had set out a spirit lamp and my surgical tools: tweezers, a scalpel, cotton, alcohol, bandages. He grew afraid when I shut the door and shone the lamp on him.

"I don't want you to do it," he said. "You don't know anything about this. You said you'd never seen this thing before."

I said, "Do you want to die?"

He sobbed and lay flat on the bed. I bent over him to begin. The maggots had grown larger, some had broken the skin, and their ugly heads stuck out like beads. I lanced the worst boil, between his shoulder blades. Jerry cried out and arched his back, but I kept digging and prodding, and I found that heat made it simpler. If I held my cigarette lighter near the wound the maggot wriggled, and by degrees, I eased it out. The danger lay in their breaking: if I pulled too hard some would be left in the boil to decay, and that I said would kill him.

By the end of the afternoon I had removed only twenty or so, and Jerry had fainted from the pain. He woke at nightfall. He looked at the saucer beside the bed and saw the maggots jerking in it — they had worked themselves into a white knot — and he screamed. I had to hold him until he calmed down. And then I continued.

I kept at it until very late. And I must admit that it gave me a certain pleasure. It was not only that Jerry deserved to suffer for his deceit — and his suffering was that of a condemned man; but also what I told him had been true: this was a startling discovery for me, as an entomologist. I had never seen such creatures before.

It was after midnight when I stopped. My hand ached, my eyes hurt from the glare, and I was sick to my stomach. Jerry had gone to sleep. I switched off the light and left him to his nightmares.

*   *   *

He was slightly better by morning. He was still pale, and the opened boils were crusted with blood, but he had more life in him than I had seen for days. And yet he was brutally scarred. I think he knew this: he looked as if he had been whipped.

"You saved my life," he said.

"Give it a few days," I said.

He smiled. I knew what he was thinking. Like all liars — those people who behave like human flies on our towering credulity — he was preparing his explanation. But this would be a final reply: he was preparing his escape.

"I'm leaving," he said. "I've got some money — and there's a night bus — ". He stopped speaking and looked at my desk. "What's that?"

It was the dish of maggots, now as full as a rice pudding.

"Get rid of them!"

"I want to study them," I said. "I think I've earned the right to do that. But I'm off to morning assembly — what shall I tell Inky?"

"Tell him I might have this cold for a long time."

He was gone when I got back to the house; his room had been emptied, and he'd left me his books and his tennis racket with a note. I made what explanations I could. I told the truth: I had no idea where he had gone. A week later, Petra went back to Rhodesia, but she told me she would be back. As we chatted over the fence I heard Jerry's voice: *She's screaming for it.* I said, "We'll go horseback riding."

"Super!"

The curse of the white worm: Jerry had believed me. But it was the curse of impatience — he had been impatient to get rid of Ameena, impatient for Petra, impatient to put on a shirt that had not been ironed. What a pity it was that he was not around when the maggots hatched, to see them become flies I had never seen. He might have admired the way I expertly pickled some and sealed others in plastic and mounted twenty of them on a tray.

And what flies they were! It was a species that was not in any book, and yet the surprising thing was that in spite of their differently shaped wings (like a Muslim woman's cloak) and the shape of their bodies (a slight pinch above the thorax, giving them rather attractive waists), their life cycle was the same as many others of their kind: they laid their eggs on laundry and these larvae hatched at body heat and burrowed into the skin to mature. Of course, laundry was always ironed — even drip-dry shirts — to kill them. Everyone who knew Africa knew that.

CLAPHAM JUNCTION

"THE SATISFACTION of working snails out of shells," said Cox, "is the satisfaction of successfully picking one's nose." He had been hunched over his plate, screwing the gray meat out of the glistening yellow-black shell. Now he looked up and said, "Don't you think so?"

Mrs. Etterick looked at him sideways. She said, "I'm glad Gina is upstairs."

But her expression told him that he had scored. Encouraged, he said, "A horrible, private sort of relief. Like finding exactly what you need at Woolworth's. A soap dish. Those plastic discs you put under chair legs so they won't dent the carpet."

"Now you've gone too far," said Mrs. Etterick.

Rudge said, "And how is dear Gina? Is she any better?"

"She seems happy. In that sense she is better," said Mrs. Etterick. "But hers is not the sort of affliction that can be cured in a place like Sunbury. She is so very backward in some ways. I say 'affliction' — but that doesn't describe it. She is like a different racial type altogether, like someone from a primitive tribe. Terribly sweet, but terribly uncivilized. I sometimes think what a pity it was, when she was born that — "

Mrs. Etterick faced her snails and reproached herself with a shudder.

"There is a kind of light in her face," Rudge said. "I noticed it when she let me in tonight. She was standing there like a very serious head prefect."

"She is nearly thirty," said Mrs. Etterick. "I still have to wash her face and comb her hair. Head prefects, in my experience, can manage those things."

Cox had finished his snails. He was smiling at Rudge.

Rudge said, "I meant there was a gentleness about her, something distinctly proper."

"She broke a vase this afternoon. She kept asking me where she should put it. I could hardly hear her. She gets very exasperated, awfully flustered. I came down the stairs. When she saw me she started to juggle it. They don't have the same joints in their fingers that we do. Then it went crash." Mrs. Etterick dropped a snail shell with her tongs, as if intending to give drama to what Gina had done. She said, "I think she did it on purpose."

"Perhaps a plea for love," Rudge said.

"Rubbish," said Mrs. Etterick. "That vase cost less than a pound."

Cox began to laugh. He was not a man given to expression, but the laugh accomplished his purpose; it complimented Mrs. Etterick and it mocked Rudge. But it also slewed in his throat, and it was loud with greed.

Rudge said, "I've always wanted a daughter. Particularly at a time of year like this. Christmas. It seems part of the season."

"You sound like her," said Mrs. Etterick, rising, collecting the plates. Rudge rose to help her, but she waved him aside, saying that she could manage.

Cox rocked his chair back and yawned. Then he said, "Those snails were marvelous."

"It's a sort of kit," said Mrs. Etterick. "You get snail mince and empty shells in a box. You stuff the shells and heat them through. It's really very simple."

She returned with a casserole dish on which spills of juice had been baked black on the rim. "Cassoulet," she said. "I put it in the oven this morning. I had to spend the day shopping."

"When I didn't see you in your office," said Cox, "I thought you were home, cooking. Now I don't feel so guilty."

"I couldn't face the party."

"It was all secretaries," Rudge said.

"So you noticed," Cox replied.

"I noticed you," said Rudge.

Cox turned to Mrs. Etterick. "Are you going away for Christmas?"

"My plans are still pretty fluid," she said. "Gina's been on at me to make a week of it. That's a fairly grim prospect."

Cox said, "So you might be alone?"

"I'm not sure."

The two men ate in silence. Upstairs, the radio was loud.

Mrs. Etterick said, "Gina's transistor. I decided to give her her present early. She *will* leave the door open."

Cox said, "I hate Christmas."

Mrs. Etterick filled Rudge's glass with claret and said, "You'll be spending Christmas here in London, then?"

"I have an open invitation in Scotland," Rudge said.

"Snow in the Highlands!" said Cox.

"Rain, more likely. The Lowlands — Peebles," said Rudge. "It's my mother."

"Will you go?" asked Mrs. Etterick.

Rudge stared, holding his knife and fork, and with hunger on his face he seemed on the point of cutting a slice from Mrs. Etterick's white forearm and stuffing it into his mouth. He lowered the implements and in a subdued voice said, "That depends."

"Such a lovely house you have, Diana. I hadn't realized you'd such a passion for oriental art. It's all frightfully dazzling." Cox had finished eating and had lit a cigarette. "Is this an ashtray, or a funerary urn?"

"Both," said Mrs. Etterick. "Yes, we were in Thailand. That's where I lost my husband. He was at the university."

"An academic in the family," said Cox. "Forgive me — I wasn't mocking."

"He was the bursar."

"Was it one of these tropical diseases?" asked Rudge.

"Yes," said Mrs. Etterick. "She was about twenty, one of these heartless Chinese girls that are determined to leave Thailand. I can't tell you how beautiful she was. She set about him like an infection. They're in Australia now. I imagine she's quite bored with Richard these days. I got the Buddhas, the bronzes, the porcelain. You could pick it up for next to nothing then. The looters, you know. It was all looters."

Rudge said, "I was thinking of staying in town over Christmas. Perhaps taking in a show or a concert. Last year, I saw Verdi's *Otello*. Placido Domingo. Overwhelming. I've always wanted to attend the carol service at Saint Paul's. Something traditional."

"Last year," Cox said, "Boxing Day, I went up to the Odeon in Holloway and saw a double bill. *The Godfather* — both parts. Best afternoon I'd spent in ages. Place was full of yobs."

Mrs. Etterick said, "I'd like to close my eyes and open them and discover it's January."

"I'd like to spend the next eight days in bed, watching rubbish on television and eating buttered toast. I mean, really pig it until London's back to normal," Cox said.

"In Bangkok, you never knew it was Christmas. The heat was dreadful — I loved it. And Gina had an amah then. Amazing, isn't it? They were both seventeen, only the amah was about a foot shorter. But she kept Gina well in check. There were parties, but none of this bogus nostalgia. All the Christmas decorations were in the massage parlors and the brothels — well, that's what Richard told me. The Americans carried on, of course. But they would."

"I had no idea there was another Far East hand at Alliance," Cox said.

"Another?" said Mrs. Etterick.

"I was in Malaya during the war," Cox said. "It was long before your time. But I stayed on. I rather enjoyed the Japanese surrender. It was a terrible shambles. They handed Kota Bahru over to me — can you imagine?"

Rudge said, "There is so much that we have yet to understand about the East. Yes, I suppose one can treat it all as a great joke. Those funny little people. But our destiny lies in the hands of those funny little people."

"They go out of their way to insult us," Cox said. "They make no serious attempt to understand us. Never did. I have always taken the view that we should offer them all the friendly attention they offer us. I mean, if they turf out our people we should immediately turf out one of theirs. Only language they understand."

"Who are we talking about?" asked Rudge.

"Orientals," Cox said.

"You lump them all together."

"My dear boy, they lump *us* all together. We are westerners, they are orientals."

Rudge said, "Did Shiner ever tell you that terrible story about his visit to the Canton Trade Fair? It was when Alliance sent that industrial software delegation over, about three years ago."

Cox said, "I never speak to Shiner. I don't like his eyes, or his software, for that matter."

"His secretary had that nervous breakdown," said Mrs. Etterick. "That spoke volumes."

"It makes no difference whether we like Shiner or not," Rudge said. "The story still stands."

Cox said, "Get on with it, then. I can see there is no way of stopping you."

"Apparently they went all out to impress our delegation," Rudge said. "Took them to spindle factories, steel mills, hydroelectric plants. Well, you know. Then they took them to a model commune. The interpreter got hold of the headman and translated what he said. 'In five years our cotton acreage has risen fiftyfold,' says the headman. 'We have increased production of vegetable fiber by two hundred percent.' Shiner was terribly impressed. They inspected the schools, the electricity plant, the kitchens. All this time, the headman is raving about the progress they've made and saying how happy everyone is. 'Under the wise leadership of Chairman Mao, we have gone from strength to strength.' Shiner signed the visitors' book and said he'd have to leave. 'No,' said the headman, 'there is one more thing I must show you.' Out of politeness, Shiner agreed. Then there was a bit of by-play between the interpreter and the headman. The headman said that he wanted to take Shiner upstairs, but that the staircase was very narrow and the room was small and so forth. The interpreter relented, and off they went, Shiner and the headman, to inspect this attic."

"Now comes the interesting part," Cox said.

"There was a cradle in this attic. The headman leaned over to Shiner and said, 'That is my daughter.' He spoke in English! Shiner was astonished, but before he could recover himself, the headman had picked up the child. He was frantic. He put the child in Shiner's arms and said, 'Take her with you! Please, take her away from here! You must do this! She has no future here in China!' "

"Is this an ashtray, too?" said Cox to Mrs. Etterick. But she was squinting at Rudge.

"Shiner never said a word," said Rudge. "He simply put the child back into the cradle and took himself away. But he told me he was really quite shaken by it."

"I'd divide anything Shiner says by ten," said Cox.

"The story is true," Rudge said. "There were others present. He had witnesses."

"But there were only two of them in the attic. You said so."

"I think it is a heart-rending story," Rudge said. He appealed to Mrs. Etterick. "I sometimes wonder what I would have done if I'd been in Shiner's position."

"If you'd had any sense you'd have taken the next rickshaw out of the place," Cox said.

"I'd like to think I was the sort of man who could get that infant out of the country."

"And where would you bring this ashen-faced tot? To England? What future would she have here?"

Mrs. Etterick said, "Gina was very happy in Bangkok. She hasn't been nearly so happy since."

"I have nothing so dramatic to offer as Shiner's story," Cox said. "I wasn't on a company swan to the Canton Trade Fair. I was in the army, and Kota Bahru was about the grimmest place I'd ever seen. I couldn't imagine why the Japanese had wanted to capture it, or why we were so bloody keen to get it back. But I was an officer and I was put in charge of the reoccupation. What made me think of this? I suppose it was your mention of looters, Diana. After the surrender, Malaya was swarming with looters and Kota Bahru seemed to have more than its fair share. They made me livid. They spent the war hiding behind trees while British soldiers were dying in battle or rotting in prison camps. One day, I was driving along in my jeep. This was just outside of town. I saw a looter running across the road with an enormous great sack. I slammed on the brakes and hopped out of the jeep. And I suppose I yelled at him to stop — I really can't remember. It all happened so fast. I then took out my pistol — the chap was still beetling away with his sack — and fired. One shot. The man fell dead."

"That's horrible," Rudge said.

"I was afraid," Cox said, "that he might still be alive. He was lying there. I couldn't see any blood. I wasn't even a good shot! I thought he was faking — the way animals pretend they're dead. He had flopped over so quickly, just like a rabbit. I kept my pistol aimed at him as I walked over to him, and then I saw that I had got him right through the heart. The blood had started to clot on his blouse. It was a woman's blouse. I imagine he had stolen that, too."

"What a thing to have on your conscience," Rudge said.

"Precisely," Cox said. "I thought I'd have a terrible night. But not a bit! I went back to my bungalow and ate a huge meal and then slept like a baby."

Mrs. Etterick said, "And I'll bet everyone blamed you afterward and said you hadn't any right."

"Some fools did, but I don't suppose anyone really cared."

"There's no dessert," Mrs. Etterick said. "I have some fresh fruit and some cheese, if anyone's interested."

"I'll help you clear away these things," said Cox.

"Leave them, please, Austin," Mrs. Etterick said. "I rather like sitting in the rubble."

Rudge said, "Some years, there's lots of snow in Peebles." He stood up. "I ought to be off," he said. "Are you going? We're both crossing the river. We could share a taxi."

"I'm going to linger a bit in the rubble," Cox said. "But don't let me hold you up." Now he looked at Mrs. Etterick, "Or would it be simpler if we both left?"

* * *

Though it was almost eight-thirty, it was still dark the following morning as the mother and daughter walked down St. John's Hill to Clapham Junction. Mrs. Etterick was brisk and silent, keeping four steps ahead of Gina, who was unusually talkative for this early hour. Passing the sweet shops on the hill, Gina remarked that they might buy their chocolate oranges on the way back; at the Granada, Gina said they'd have to see the Disney film — perhaps tomorrow; and there were Christmas trees stacked at the flower shop: Gina fell behind, choosing one. Mrs. Etterick had not paused, or replied, and Gina had toiled on clumsy feet to catch up with her. The daughter was big, but had the stumbling round-shouldered gait of a small child. Her eyes were hooded slits in her fat solemn face and her arms swung uselessly in her sleeves.

Gina said, "After Daddy died and went to Heaven — "

Mrs. Etterick quickened her pace.

A crowd of people stood at the ticket window. Mrs. Etterick joined them. Now Gina entered the lobby.

"Mum," she said in a pleading voice. "After Daddy died — "

"You're talking much too loud," Mrs. Etterick said sharply. "You'll have to stand in the corner. Over there."

Gina lugged herself to the corner and waited, murmuring.

It was Mrs. Etterick's turn. She put her money down and leaned toward the plastic grille. "One single and one return to Sunbury, please."

THE ODD-JOB MAN

EVERY SPRING, on the first free day after exams, Lowell Bloodworth and his wife, Shelley, drove to Boston from Amherst and then flew to London. He told people he was seeing his publisher. But he had no publisher. The London visits had begun when, as an associate professor, Bloodworth was working on his edition of *The Family Letters of Wilbur Parsons*. He had brought a box of the letters, rented a room near Sloane Square, and stuck them into a thick album, working by the window with a brush and a bottle of glue; he added footnotes in ink and gave each personal observation a crimson exclamation mark. English academics mocked his enterprise. He would not be drawn, but Shelley said, "It's not easy editing the letters of a living poet." English academics said they had never heard of Parsons. Bloodworth had a reply: "The only difference between Wallace Stevens and Wilbur Parsons is that Stevens was vice president of an insurance company and Parsons was president — still is."

"Why is it," an Englishman once said to him, "American academics are forever putting their fingers down their throats and bringing up books like these?" Bloodworth had thought of asking that man to help him find an English publisher. It struck Bloodworth as odd that the mere mention of his book caused shouts of laughter in London. Especially odd since this book, brought out in America after several delays by a university press, got Lowell Bloodworth the tenure he wanted, and now he was earning thirty thousand dollars a year. But it was the salary that embarrassed him, not the book. There was an additional bonus: the *Times Literary Supplement* gave him one of Parsons's collections to review, and years afterward Bloodworth said, "I do a little writing for the *TLS*," often claiming credit for anonymous reviews he admired.

He liked London, but his links with the life of the city tended to be imaginary. There was that huge party at William Empson's. Bloodworth had gone with one of Mr. Empson's former students (who, as it turned out, had not been invited either). Bloodworth talked the whole evening to an elderly man who told malicious stories against Edith Sitwell. The stories became Bloodworth's own, and later, describing that summer to his Amherst colleagues, he said, "We spent quite a bit of time with the Empsons . . ." He appropriated gossip and gave it the length of anecdote. One summer he saw Frank Kermode across a room. In the autumn, for a colleague, he turned this glimpse into a meeting.

Nine summers, nine autumns had been spent this way; and always Bloodworth regretted that he had so little to show after such long flights. He craved something substantial: a literary find, an eminent friend, a famous enemy. Inevitably his rivalries were departmental; the department had grown, and for the past few years Bloodworth's younger colleagues, all of whom flew to England in June, had come back with similar stories. In the warm, early autumn afternoons they would meet at Bloodworth's "Little Britain" on the Shutesbury Road; the wives in Liberty prints swapping play titles, the children jerking at Hamlys' toys, and the men discussing London as if it were no larger or more complicated than Amherst itself: "Leavis is looking a lot older . . . ," "We saw Iris Murdoch in Selfridge's . . . ," "Cal's divorce is coming through . . ." This last remark from Siggins, whose preposterous anecdotes Bloodworth suspected were nimble parodies of his own: lately, Bloodworth had felt (the word was Parsons's) outgunned.

This was the first year the Bloodworths had spent their English vacation outside London. They were flushed from Sloane Square by the department. On their second day in London they met Cliff Margoulies on Pont Street. He had a story about Angus Wilson. That afternoon, they bumped into Siggins at the Byron exhibition. Bloodworth said he was just leaving. The next day he had gone back to the Byron exhibition and seen Arvin Prizeman: there was just no escaping them. He ran into Milburn at the Stoppard play, and Shelley had seen the Hoffenbergs at Biba's. Each encounter was alarming, producing a keen embarrassment Bloodworth disguised unwillingly in heartiness. The prospect of a summer of these chance meetings made Bloodworth cringe, and so, at the end of their first week, the Bloodworths took a train to the village of Hooke, in Kent, where they rented a small cottage ("Batcombe") for the remainder of their vacation.

It was not a coincidence that a mile from this village was the house of the American poet Walter Van Bellamy, who had been living in England since the war. Bellamy was an irascible man of about seventy who had known both Pound and Eliot — and been praised by them — and who (though the airfare to New York was less than his well-publicized phone bill) described himself as an exile. Bloodworth was not the first American to get the idea of going to Hooke with the intention of making Walter Van Bellamy's acquaintance; there had been others — poets, Ph.D. candidates, anthologists — but invariably they were turned away. Out of spite they reported how they had found Bellamy drunk. The more Bellamy protected his privacy, the more scandalous the stories became.

Bloodworth, who gave a Bellamy seminar, was anxious to verify the stories. He had often talked to Wilbur Parsons about Bellamy's influence: Parsons acknowledged the fact that Bellamy was the greater poet, but they had, Parsons said, been good friends and had once dated the same Radcliffe girl. Now, Bloodworth's ambition went beyond verifying the scandalous stories or even meeting the man. He had in mind an edition of poems that would be different from anything scholarship had so far produced. This book, "Presented by Lowell Bloodworth," would consist of poems in Bellamy's hand, photographs of work sheets and fair copies, discovered drafts, inky lyrics, all of them nobly scrawled instead of diminished by the regularity of typefaces. It would be a collector's item: Introduction by Bloodworth, Notes by Bloodworth — the sort of book got up to honor a dead poet's memory, an exhibit showing crossed-out lines, second thoughts, hasty errors in the poet's own handwriting. Bloodworth's sections, of course, would be printed in Times Roman. In his mind the book became such a finished thing that when he remembered he had not yet met the man he grew restless to see samples of his handwriting.

* * *

"I've seen him," Shelley said, several days after their arrival in Hooke. It was at the off-license. Bellamy (confirming scandal) was buying an enormous bottle of gin. The man behind the counter had said, "Will that be all, Mr. Bellamy?" and Bellamy had grunted and gone away in a car. Shelley described Bellamy closely: the hair, the walking stick, the green sweater, the car, even the brand of gin.

Bloodworth was excited. The next morning he saw the car parked near the village's cricket ground, and on the grass Bellamy was throwing a mangled ball for his dog to fetch.

"There are people," said Bloodworth, "who'd risk losing tenure to be right here at this moment."

The poet shambled after his dog.

"Say something," said Shelley.

"This is an historic moment," said Bloodworth. He added, "I mean, in my life."

"No, say something to *him*."

But Bellamy was headed in the opposite direction, flinging the ball.

"Rain," said Shelley, looking up. She spread her palms to the sky. There was a sound, far off, of thunder, and a spark of lightning from the underside of a black cloud.

Bloodworth shook out the umbrella he habitually carried in England. He said, "Bellamy doesn't have one."

The poet seemed not to notice the rain. He tramped slowly, circled by the excited dog. For a moment Bloodworth imagined Walter Van Bellamy, the American poet, struck by lightning and killed instantly while he watched from the boundary of the field. He drew grim cheer from the reflection, and saw the thunderbolt's jagged arrow enter Bellamy's head, saw the poet stagger, and himself sprinting across the cricket pitch, then kneeling: critic administering the kiss of life to poet. Bellamy's death would make an attractive article, but if Bloodworth managed to bring him back to life the poet would be grateful, and it was a short distance from lifesaver to literary executor; indeed, they were much the same.

The sun broke through the sacking of clouds, and it was then, in the barely perceptible rain, that Bloodworth ran across the grass and offered his umbrella to the poet.

"What do you want?" said Walter Van Bellamy, wheeling around, startled by Bloodworth's panting.

His ferocity did not stop Bloodworth, who said, "I thought you might need this. I happened to be passing — "

"Who's that?" said Bellamy. Shelley — her plastic raincoat flying like a cape — was making her way to where the men stood.

"That's my wife," said Bloodworth. "Shelley, I'd like you to meet Walter Van Bellamy."

"Who the hell are *you*?" demanded Bellamy.

Bloodworth introduced himself.

"I'm just going home," said Bellamy.

"We'll walk you back to your car."

Bellamy said something, but Bloodworth realized he was talking to his dog.

Bloodworth said, "Wilbur's a great friend of ours."

"Richard Wilbur?" Bellamy seemed to relax.

"Wilbur Parsons."

"Never heard of him," said Bellamy.

Bloodworth started to describe Parsons's contribution to American poetry and Bellamy's profound influence on the man ("Going back to what you said about mankind's terrible . . .").

"Say," said Bellamy, interrupting him, "do you happen to know anything about light plugs?"

"Light plugs?"

"These English plugs have three colored wires, and they just changed the goddamned colors, if you please. I've been trying to figure out which wire goes where. Ralph's never around when I want him, and I spent the whole morning trying to connect my new shaver."

"Leave it to me," said Bloodworth with energy.

"I really appreciate that," said Bellamy. "Come over this afternoon around drink time. Bring your wife if you want. This plug's driving me nuts." Bellamy helped his dog into the car and without another word sped down the road.

"Talk about luck," said Bloodworth.

Shelley said, "He seems kind of rude."

"You'd be rude, too, if you'd had his life. Shelley, he's got *wounds!*"

* * *

In the pub, The King's Arms, at lunchtime Bloodworth inquired about the way to Bellamy's house. The landlord started to tell him, but halfway through the explanation the door flew open and a tall muscular man came in. The man was young, but balding like a man of sixty. He wore a leather jacket, and under it a T-shirt. He grinned and ordered a beer.

"Here's the man who'll tell you the quickest way to Bellamy's," said the landlord. "Ralph, come here."

"What's the problem?" asked Ralph.

"Ralph here works for your friend Bellamy. He's the odd-job man."

"It's a husband and wife thing," said Ralph. "My wife does the housework and cooking. I do the odd jobs — gardening, that lark."

"When he feels like it," said the landlord.

"When I feels like it," said Ralph.

"I know a lot of people who'd give their right arm to work for Walter Van Bellamy," said Bloodworth.

"Not in Hooke you don't," said Ralph. He winked at the landlord. "Right, Sid?"

Bloodworth suppressed a lecture. "You were saying, the quickest way . . ."

"Oh, yeah. Here, I'll draw you a map." He made the map carefully, sketching the streets and labeling them, marking the way with arrows, noting landmarks. Bloodworth was surprised by the stubborn, conscientious way the odd-job man worked with his pencil, and when Ralph said, "I think that's worth a beer, don't you?" Bloodworth dumped change on the counter for three pints.

At half past four, the Bloodworths walked the pleasant mile along winding country roads to Bellamy's house. The house was not signposted, nor did it have a name. It was a converted farmhouse at the end of a close lane, set amid crumbling farm buildings, a roofless barn, broken sheds, and fences with no gates. They were met at the front door by a woman of about thirty with a white, suspicious face.

"Mrs. Bellamy?"

"She's in Italy."

Bloodworth explained his errand. The woman said, "Wait here." She closed the door in their faces and bounded through the house; they heard her on the stairs. Then she returned and led them to an upstairs room, where Bellamy sat at a cluttered table. On the table were papers, unopened letters, a stack of books, a wine bottle, a glass, and the electric shaver with its flex exposed.

"I'll have that fixed in a jiffy," said Bloodworth. He lifted the shaver and, pretending to examine it, looked past it to the swatches of paper with their blocks of blue stanzas. He was glad, but it was not the simple thrill he had once invented for himself ("Walter was showing me some of his rough drafts . . ."): in this script he saw his finished book, that album of scribbles.

"Doris," said Bellamy to the woman, "bring a couple of glasses, will you?"

Bloodworth took the plug apart, stripped the wires, and said, "Looks like you're hard at work."

But Bellamy was staring at the plug. "I don't understand why they don't sell the shaver with the plug on. I suppose that's too simple."

Bloodworth repeated, "Looks like you're hard at work. New book?"

"What's that?" Bellamy said. "Oh, fiddling around. My wife's out of town. That usually gets me writing."

"Lowell's a writer," said Shelley.

"Robert Lowell?" said Bellamy.

"No — me," said Bloodworth. "I do a little teaching on the side to pay the grocery bill, that sort of thing. Well, I mentioned my Parsons edition this morning. I like to *present* a poet, get him an audience. Some people call it criticism, but I think of it as presentation. And" — Bloodworth bit a length of plastic from one of the wires — "I do quite a bit of reviewing."

"You don't say," said Bellamy.

Bloodworth saw he had not roused him. He took a breath. "I've even done some reviews of your work."

"That's funny," said Bellamy, turning from the plug to Bloodworth, "I don't recall your name."

"It wasn't signed. Actually it was for the *TLS*, so you could hardly be expected — "

"The *TLS*? Was it about a year ago, that review of *Hooked*?"

Bloodworth did not hesitate. He stuck the last wire into the plug and said, "Yup."

Bellamy struggled to his feet and snatched the plug out of Bloodworth's hands. He weighed it like a grenade — Bloodworth thought he might throw it — and said fiercely, "Get out of here this minute and take your wife with you. Doris!" (She stood in the doorway, a wineglass in each hand.) "See these people out. You, sir," he said to Bloodworth, "are over-certain to the point of libel, and if there's one thing I will not stand — "

Bloodworth did not wait to hear what it was. Bellamy was a big man, and enraged he looked even bigger. There was a story that Ezra Pound had taught Bellamy to box. The fact was pertinent, for it is well known that Pound had sparred with Hemingway. The Bloodworths bolted.

At the road they paused for a last look at the house. The house was lighted; the lingering storm had darkened the late afternoon. But as they watched, the lights went out, all at once, just like that. And they heard within the house the poet howl.

"The plug," said Bloodworth. "I think I've made a mess of that too."

*   *   *

Bloodworth thought of writing Bellamy a letter, explaining everything. But it had gone too far for that, and Shelley said, "Let's forget it, Lowey. It was a horrible mistake. There's no sense crying about it. We can go back to London and see some plays."

"And Siggins, and Margoulies, and Prizeman . . ." Bloodworth flinched: a return to London was a return to the department.

"But we can't stay here. Not after that."

Bloodworth said, "I hate to leave empty-handed. Let's give it a few more days."

They saw no more of Bellamy. Bloodworth watched for his car, his dog, for any sign of him; but the poet had withdrawn to his farmhouse. Bloodworth hiked through the damp fields, hoping to meet him, and he imagined a situation in which he could undo all his bungling. He might happen upon the poet drowning, or lamed by a fall, or cursing a blowout Bloodworth could fix. It might rain again: a crippling thunderbolt. No opportunity presented itself. And Bloodworth walked alone, for Shelley had come down with a cold. She sat in "Batcombe" with the electric fire on, reading a Dick Francis she'd found on the bookshelf.

One evening, leaving Shelley at the cottage, Bloodworth went to The King's Arms and saw Ralph. Ralph said, "If you know what's good for you, you won't come over to the farm!"

"I guess he's pretty mad."

"He's been screaming his head off for the past three days," said Ralph. "I don't know why, but he takes it out on Doris and me. I mean, I don't care myself. I tell him to his face to leave me alone. But not my wife. She's the quiet type. Just sits there and takes it. He's a bastard, he is. You Yanks are all alike."

Bloodworth didn't know what to say. Finally he said, "Bellamy is a very gifted poet. But his reputation has suffered. I wanted to help him."

Ralph said, "You're a great help. He had to get an electrician in. For the lights. You fused 'em."

"An American poet," said Bloodworth, still thinking of Bellamy, "needs an American critic, an American audience."

Ralph said, "Hey, is it true that one third of all the dog food in America is eaten by human beings?"

"No," said Bloodworth.

"I heard that somewhere," said Ralph. "The thing is, I suppose, my wife has no sense of smell. She burns things. What

I'm trying to say is, it's hard to be a cook if you can't smell."

"Funny. I'd never thought of that."

"Some people are born that way. Old Bellamy shouts about his food — says it's too salty, or overdone, or underdone. My wife's disabled and he shouts. Sympathy? Not him — just poems."

"Why do you put up with it, then?"

"I take a pride in my work," said Ralph. "And you can't beat the money; Bellamy's rolling in it. You buggers make a fortune. But Christ, *I* could write the stuff he does! Ever seen it?"

"I teach it," said Bloodworth.

"It's rubbish," said Ralph. He recited in a lilting voice, " 'I was walking down the road. I seen two cows. The sky turned green. My uncle don't like me. Oh-oh-oh. I remember them cows. Hum-hum-hum. My heart she's shaking like a big fat drum.' "

"He never wrote that."

"Oh no? I *seen* it. The most awful crap. I could do it myself. I *do* do it — tried it once or twice, pretty good stuff. Pomes." Ralph grinned. "You know what I think? I think he gets people to write it. He's got so much money, and these sickly looking buggers are always sloping around the place — 'Don't touch this, don't touch that.' "

"You haven't read any of his books," said Bloodworth.

"The hell I haven't," said Ralph. "And I've done a tidy sight more than that. I've read the stuff on his desk, all the scribbly papers. 'My heart was walking down the road and seen two fat cows,' that stuff. 'Chickenzola, how's your father.' I've read the lot. It stinks."

"I don't believe you."

"I don't care if you believe me or not," said Ralph. "If I wasn't making money off him I'd go and give some lectures. Rent a church hall somewhere and say, 'Well, here's the truth about your so-called great poet, Mr. Bellamy — ' That'd shake him!"

Bloodworth said, "Suppose I was to say to you, man to man, 'Prove it'? What would you say to that?"

"I'd say, 'Why?'"

"Let's say I'm interested, I want to give you a chance," said Bloodworth. "I know what you've been through."

"It would cost you something."

"How much?"

"More than ten quid, I can tell you that."

"Let's say fifteen," said Bloodworth.

"Let's say thirty," said Ralph.

"You drive a hard bargain."

"Like I say, I'm me own man. My wife, she just takes it from him. Bellamy thinks an odd-job man is someone you shout at, but I do my work and I shout back. I take a pride in my work — whatever I do, I take a pride in it."

Ralph, Bloodworth could see, was three-parts drunk. He wanted to cut the business short. He said, "Now let's get this straight. What you're going to do is bring me two or three examples of his bad poetry . . ."

"Listen," said Ralph, "make it fifty quid and I'll bring you the whole bloody lot in a bushel basket!"

That evening Bloodworth told his wife Ralph's extraordinary story. Shelley was fearful, but Bloodworth said, "After what he's done to us? Thrown us out of his house — and we went over there with the best of intentions. I tell you, he deserves what's coming to him."

"I didn't like the look of that Ralph. He's probably wrong."

"Probably," said Bloodworth. "But think of the manuscripts, work sheets! Shelley, they're gold! And what if he's right?"

* * *

Ralph was not in The King's Arms the next day. Bloodworth stopped in at lunchtime, then returned at six-thirty and stayed until closing. He watched an interminable darts game, he made himself ill on cider, and briefly he wondered if the whole affair might not be the blunder Shelley feared it was. But the critic's rules were not the poet's, and what the poet called ruthlessness the critic might give another name. Bloodworth sympathized with Ralph, the odd-job man; he saw the similarity in his tasks and the critic's: they received orders from the man whose poetry had earned him privileges, and stood at the margins of the poet's world, listening for a shout, waiting for a poem. But what critic had marched forward and snatched a poem from under the poet's nose? None had dared — until now. Bloodworth saw himself on the frontier of criticism, where there was danger, and not the usual tact required, but elaborate deceits and stratagems, odd ways of doing odd jobs. He went to bed with these thoughts, though Shelley woke him throughout the night with her coughing.

"It's not like Ralph to miss a day," said Sid, the landlord, the next day.

Bloodworth said, "It's not important." He wondered if Ralph had betrayed him to Bellamy, and he knew a full minute of panic.

He met Ralph after closing time on the road. Ralph said, "Running away, are you?"

"I thought you weren't coming."

"It's all in here," said Ralph. He slapped his shirtfront. Bloodworth heard the sound of paper wrinkling at the stomach of the shirt. He was excited. His Introduction would be definitive. The book would be boxed. It might cost twenty dollars. Ralph said, "Let's go somewhere private."

They chose the churchyard, a shield of gravestones. Ralph said, "My wife was off yesterday. She gets these depressions. I might as well be frank. It's her tits, see. I don't understand women. I keep telling her they're not supposed to stick out. Look around, I says, lots of women have the same thing. But she — "

"What about the poems?" Bloodworth said.

"Don't rush me," said Ralph. "You don't care about any-body's problems but your own, do you? Just like old Bellamy."

"We're taking the evening train."

"First the money."

Bloodworth peeled off five five-pound notes and counted five more ones into Ralph's dirty hand.

Ralph said, "Why not make it forty? You're rolling in it."

"We agreed on thirty." Bloodworth hated the odd-job man for putting him through this.

"Have it your way." Ralph undid the buttons on his shirt and took out a creased brown envelope. "I hope you appreciate all the work I put into this. It seemed a lot of trouble to go to, but I said to Doris, 'Thirty quid is thirty quid.' " He handed the envelope to Bloodworth.

"I'm glad you're a man of your word," said Bloodworth.

"Well, you seemed to want them awful bad."

Bloodworth shook the hand of the odd-job man and hurried to "Batcombe" to tell Shelley. But partly from fear, and partly from superstition, he did not open the envelope until he was on the train and rolling through the Kent hopfields. At first he thought he had been swindled; the folded sheets, about ten of them, looked blank. But they were only blank on one side. On the other side were the collapsing rectangles of typed stanzas, lines which broke and sloped, words so badly typed they had humps and troughs. And there was a letter: *I hope you aprecate all the work I put into this but a deals a deal altho it take me a whole day to type up this stuff and any time you want some more lets see the colour of your money! Yours faithfully, R. Tunnel. P.S. I enclosed herewith one I wrote meself so you can compare.*

But the drunken typing and misspelling that made them valueless to Bloodworth did not disguise the beauty of the lines. Reading them made his eyes hurt. He turned quickly to Ralph's own poem, which began,

The odd-job man thats me
Messing around in my bear feat
Can make a stie from some tree
Raise up pigs for the meat.

The polecat, he thought, and his anger stayed with him for four English days. But back in Amherst he recovered himself, and when the department met for drinks and showed their trophies — Waterford crystal, a Daniell engraving of Wick, a first edition of *Howards End* — Bloodworth brought out his folder and said, "I've got some unpublished Bellamy variants in here, and the work of a new poet; he's terribly regional but quite exciting." Prizeman squinted; Margoulies smirked; the others stared. He shuffled the summer's result, but as he passed the poems around to convince the men, it struck him that he had the oddest job of all.

PORTRAIT OF A LADY

A HUNDRED TIMES, Harper had said to himself: *I am in Paris.*
At first he had whispered it with excitement, but as the days
passed he began mouthing it in a discouraged way, almost in
disbelief, in the humiliated tones of a woman who realizes that
her lover is not ever going to turn up. His doubt of the city
made him doubt himself.

He was in Paris waiting for a sum of money in cash to be
handed to him. He was expected to carry this bundle back to
the States. That was the whole of his job: he was a courier.
The age of technology demanded this simple human service,
a return to romance: he tucked his business under his arm —
the money, the message — as men had a century ago. It was a
delicate matter; also, it was illegal.

Harper had been hired for his loyalty and resourcefulness.
His employer demanded honesty, but implied that cunning
would be required of him. He had impressed his employer because he wasn't hungry and wasn't looking for work. And, a
recent graduate of Harvard Business School, Harper was passionate about real estate investment. Afterward he discovered
that real estate investment was carrying a flat briefcase with
eighty-five thousand dollars in used hundreds from an Iranian
in Paris to an office in Boston, to invest in an Arizona super-

market or a chain of hamburger joints. They probably didn't even eat hamburgers, the Iranians — probably against their religion; so much was. Money (he, from Harvard Business School, had to be told this) shows up in a luggage x-ray at an airport security check as innocently as laundry, like so many folded hankies.

I am in Paris. But his first sight of the place gave him the only impression that stayed with him: there were parts of Paris that resembled Harvard Square.

He had told his wife that he would be back by the following weekend, and had flown to Paris on Sunday believing that he could pick up the cash on Monday. A day to loaf, then home on Wednesday, and his surprised wife seeing him grinning in the doorway would say, "So soon?"

He had not known that Monday was a holiday; this he spent furiously walking, wishing the day away. On Tuesday, he found Undershaw's office closed — Undershaw was the Iranian's agent, British: everyone got a slice. Harper's briefcase felt ridiculously light. That afternoon he tried the telephone. The line was busy; that made him hopeful. He took a taxi to the office but found it as he had that morning, locked, with no message on the dusty glass. On Wednesday he canceled his flight and tried again. This time there was a secretary in the outer office. She did not know Undershaw's name; she was temporary, she explained. Harper left a message, marked it *Urgent* and returned to his hotel near Les Invalides and waited for the phone to ring. Then he regretted that he had left his number, because it obliged him to stay in his room for the call. There was no call. He tried to ring his wife, but failed; he wondered if the phone was broken. Thursday he wasted on three trips to the office. Each time, the secretary smiled at him and he thought he saw pity in her eyes. He became awkward under her gaze, aware that a certain frenzy showed in his rumpled clothes.

"I will take your briefcase," she said. She was French, a bit buck-toothed and angular, not what he had expected.

Harper handed it over. Not realizing its lightness until it was too late, she juggled it and almost dropped it. Harper wondered whether he had betrayed his errand by disclosing the secret of its emptiness. A man with an empty briefcase must have a shady scheme.

The street door opened and a man entered. Harper guessed this might be Undershaw; but no, the fellow was young and a moment later Harper knew he was American — something about the tortoise-shell frames, the new raincoat, the wide-open face, the way he sat with his feet apart, his shoes and the way he tapped them. Brisk apology and innocent arrogance inhabited the same body. Still sitting, he spoke to the secretary in French. She replied in English. He gave her his name — it sounded to Harper like "Bumgarner." He turned to Harper and said, "Great city."

Harper guessed that he himself had been appraised. He said, "Very nice."

Bumgarner looked at his watch, did a calculation on his fingers, and said, "I was hoping to get to the Louvre this afternoon."

He is going to say, You can spend a week there and still not see everything.

But Bumgarner said, "What part of the States are you from?"

Harper told him: Boston. It required less explanation than Melrose.

"I'm from Denver," Bumgarner said, and before Harper could praise it, Bumgarner went on, "I'm over here on a poetry grant. National Endowment for the Arts."

"You write poems?" But Harper thought of his taxes, paying for this boy's poems, the glasses, the new raincoat.

Bumgarner smiled. "I've published quite a number. I'll have enough for a collection soon."

The secretary stared at them, seeing them rattling away in their own language. Bumgarner seemed to be addressing her as well as Harper.

"I've been working on a long poem ever since I got here. It was going to be simple, but it's become the history of Europe, and in a way kind of autobiographical."

"How long have you been in Paris?"

"Two semesters."

Harper thought: *Doesn't that just sum it up.*

"Are you interested in poetry?" Bumgarner asked.

"I read the usual things at college. Yeats, Pound, Eliot. 'April is the cruellest month.'" Bumgarner appeared to be waiting for him to say something more. Harper said, "There's a lot of naive economic theory in Pound."

"I mean modern poetry."

"Isn't that modern? Pound? Eliot?"

Bumgarner said, "Eliot's kind of a back number."

And Harper was offended. He had liked Eliot and found it a relief from marketing and accountancy courses; even a solace.

"What do you think of Europe?" Bumgarner asked.

"That's a tough one, like, 'Is science good?'" But seeing that Bumgarner looked mocked and wary, Harper added, "I haven't seen much more than my hotel and this office. I can't say."

"Old Europe," said Bumgarner. "James thought it corrupted you — Daisy Miller, Lambert Strether. I've been trying to figure it out. But it does do something to you. The freedom. All the history. The outlook."

Harper said, "I can't imagine any place that has more freedom than the States."

"Ever been to Colorado?"

"No," said Harper. "But I'll bet Europeans go. And for the same reason that characters in Henry James used to come here. To escape, find freedom, live a different life. Listen, this is a pretty stuffy place."

"Depends," Bumgarner said. "I met a French girl. We're living together. That's why I'm here. I mean, I have to see this lawyer. My wife and I have decided to go our separate ways."

"Sorry to hear it." *He will go home*, thought Harper, *and he will regret his folly here.*

"It's not like that. We're going to make a clean break. We'll still be friends. We'll sell the house in Boulder. We don't have any kids."

Harper said, "Is this a lawyer's office?"

"Sure. Are you in the wrong place?"

"Anywhere away from home is the wrong place," said Harper. "I'm in brokerage. I haven't fallen in love yet. As a matter of fact, I'm dying to leave. Is Undershaw your lawyer?"

"I don't know Undershaw. Mine's Haebler — Swiss. Friend of a friend." Then Bumgarner said, "Give Paris a chance."

"Paris is an idea, but not a new one," said Harper. "I tried to call my wife. The phones don't work. Where do these people park? The restaurants cost an arm and a leg. Call this a city?"

Bumgarner laughed in a patronizing way; he didn't argue. It interested Harper to discover that there were still Americans — poets — finding Paris magical. But this poet was getting a free ride: who was paying? Only businessmen and subsidized students could afford the place. Harper had had a meal at a small restaurant the previous day. The portions were tiny, the waiter was rude, the tables were jammed together, his knees ached from the forced confinement. The meal had cost him forty-seven dollars, with wine. No wonder poets had credit cards. It was a world he understood, but not one that he had expected.

Soon after, a tall man entered: Bumgarner's lawyer. Recognizing him, Bumgarner galloped after him. Harper was annoyed that the poet had shown so little interest in him, and *Eliot's kind of a back number* had stung him. The divorce: he would make it into a poem, deal with it like a specimen in a box and ask to be excused. But the other things — the dead phones, the restaurants, the bathtubs that couldn't take your big end, the pillow bolster that was hard as a log, the expense account, the credit card — they couldn't be poems. Too messy; they didn't rhyme. *Go home!* Harper wanted to scream at Bumgarner. *Europe's more boring than Canada!*

The secretary made a sorrowful click of her tongue when Harper rose to go. She had to remind him that he had left his briefcase; empty, it hardly seemed to matter. He was thinking about his wife.

On Friday, Undershaw rang him at ten-thirty, moments before Harper, who had started sleeping late — it was boredom — was preparing to leave his hotel room. Undershaw said he had been out of town, but this was not an apology.

"I've come for the merchandise," said Harper. He wanted to say, *I've wasted a week hanging around for you to appear.* He said, "I'd like to pick up the bundle today."

"Out of the question."

Harper tried to press him, but gently: the matter was illegal. Undershaw said, "These things take time. I won't be able to do much before next week."

"Monday?"

"I can't be that definite," said Undershaw. "I'll leave a message at your hotel."

No, thought Harper. But he could not protest. He was a courier, no more than that. Undershaw did not owe him any explanation.

Harper had come to the city with one task to perform, and as he had yet to perform it his imagination wouldn't work. He had concentrated his mind on this one thing; thwarted, he could think of nothing else. He was on the hook. His boss had sent him here to hang. Paris seemed very small.

Waiting in Paris reminded Harper of his childhood, which was a jumpy feeling of interminable helplessness. And childhood was another country, too, one governed like this by secretive people who would not explain their schemes to him. He had suspected as a child that there were rules he did not know. In adulthood he learned that there were no particular rules, only arbitrary courtesies. Children were not important, because they had no power and no menace: it took a man twenty-eight years to realize that. You wait; but perhaps it is better, less humiliating, if people don't know you're waiting. Children were ignorant. The strength of adulthood lay in being dignified enough not to expose this impatience. It was worse for women. Now Harper could say to his wife: *I know how you feel.*

The weekend was dreary. Sunday in a Catholic country punished atheists by pushing them into the empty streets. Harper felt unwelcome. He did not know a soul except Bumgarner, who was smug and lucky and probably in bed with his "mistress" — the poet from Colorado would have used that silly word. Harper lay on his bed alone, studying the repetitions in the patterned wallpaper, and it struck him that it is the loneliest traveler who remembers his hotel wallpaper. He was exhausted by inaction; he wanted to go home.

He had been willing to offer the city everything. There were no takers. He thought: All travelers are like aging women, now homely beauties; the strange land flirts, then jilts and makes a fool of the stranger. There is less risk, at home, in making a jackass of yourself: you know the rules there. The answer is to be ladylike about it and maintain your dignity. But he knew as he thought this that he was denying himself the calculated risks that might bring him romance and a memory to carry away. There was no hell like a stranger's Sunday.

* * *

I'll leave a message at your hotel, Undershaw had said. That was a command. So Harper loitered in the hotel on Monday, and when he was assailed by the sense that he was lurking he went out and bought a *Herald-Tribune*; then he felt truant. At five there was no message. He decided to go for a walk, and soon he discovered himself to be walking fast toward Undershaw's office.

"He is not here," the secretary said. She knew before he opened his mouth what Harper wanted.

To cover his embarrassment, Harper said, "I knew he wasn't here. I just came to say hello."

The girl smiled. She began to cram papers and envelopes and keys into her handbag.

"I thought you might want a drink," said Harper, surprising himself at his invention.

The girl tilted her head and shrugged: it was neither yes nor no. She picked up her coat and switched off the lights as she walked to the door. Still, Harper was not sure what all this meant, until with resignation she said, "We go."

At the bar — she chose it; he would never have found it in that alley — she told him her name was Claire.

Harper began describing the emptiness he had felt on Sunday, how the only thing it was possible to do was go to church.

Claire said, "I do not go to church."

"At least we've got that in common."

A man in the bar was reading a newspaper; the headline spoke of an election. Harper mentioned this.

Claire thrust forward her lower lip and said, "I am an anarchist." She pronounced the word *anarsheest*.

"Does that mean you don't take sugar?" Harper playfully moved the sugar bowl to one side as she stirred her coffee.

She said, "You have a ring." She tapped it with a pretty finger. "Are you married?"

Harper nodded and made a private vow that he would not deceive his wife.

She said, "How is it possible to be married?"

"I know," Harper said. "You don't know anyone who's happily married. Right? But how many single people are happy?"

"Americans think happiness is so important."

"What do the French think is important?"

"Money. Clothes. Sex. That is why we are always so sad."

"Always?"

"We have no humor," she said, proving it in her solemn tone of voice. "We are — how do you say — *melancholique?*"

And Harper, who knew almost no French, translated the word. Then he complimented her on her English. Claire said that she had lived for two years in London, with an English family.

He wanted her to drink. She said she only drank wine, and that with meals. He took her to a restaurant — again she chose: a narrow noisy room. Why did they all look like ticket offices? Harper stared at the young men and women in the restaurant. The men had close-cropped hair and earrings, the women were white-faced and smoked cigarettes over their food. Harper said, "There's something about this place."

Claire smiled briefly.

"That guy in the corner," Harper said. "He's gay." Claire squinted at Harper. "A pederast."

Claire glanced at the man and made a noise of agreement. Harper smiled. "A sodomite."

"No," she said. "I am a sodomite. But he is a pederast. *Un pédé.*"

"I knew there was something about this place." Harper's scalp prickled.

"You seem a bit shocked."

"Me?" Harper tried to laugh.

"Didn't you do it at school? Playing with the other boys?"

"They would have killed me. I mean, the teachers. Anyway, I didn't want to. What about you?"

She thrust out her lower lip and said, "Of course."

"And now?"

"Of course."

The food came. They ate in silence. Harper could think of nothing to say. She was an anarchist who had just disclosed that she was also a lesbian. And he? A courier with an empty briefcase, killing time. He thought of the poet Bumgarner: Paris belonged to him. Harper could not imagine the feeling, but Bumgarner would know what to say now.

"It is easier for a woman," said Claire. He guessed that she had perceived his confusion. "I don't care whether I make love to a man or a woman. Though I have a fiancé — he is a nice boy. It is the personality that matters. I like clever men and stupid women."

"That guy who was in the office the other day," Harper said. "He's a poet. He writes poems."

Claire said, "I hate poems."

It was the most passionate thing she had said so far, but it killed his ardor.

In the twilight, under a pale watery-blue sky, they walked past biscuity buildings to the river. Although this was his eighth day in Paris, Harper's yearning for home had deserted him, and he could ignore his errand, which seemed trivial to him now. He no longer felt humiliated by suspense; and another thing released him: the girl Claire, who was neither pretty nor ugly, seemed indifferent to him. It did not matter whether he slept with her or not — he felt no desire, so there could be no such thing as failure. He enjoyed this perverse freedom, walking along the left bank of the Seine, on a mild spring evening, feeling no thrill, only a complacent lack of urgency. But that was how it was, in spite of Paris; and urgency had been no help the previous week. He did not speak French. The churches and stonecrusts were familiar; he recognized them from free calendars and jigsaw puzzles and the lids of fancy cookie tins. He had never been overseas before. It was the stage set he had imagined, but he felt unrehearsed.

"I'm tired," he said, to give Claire an excuse to go home.

She shrugged as she had before, but now the gesture irritated him because she did it so well, using her shoulders and hands and sticking out her lower lip.

"I'm staying at a hotel near Les Invalides," he said. "Would you like a drink there?"

She shrugged again. This one meant yes — it was pliable and positive.

By the time they found a taxi rank it was ten-thirty. There was traffic — worse than Boston — and they did not arrive at the hotel until after eleven. The concierge stepped from behind a palm to tell Claire the bar was closed.

Harper said, "We can drink in my room," although he had nothing there to drink.

In the room, Harper filled a tumbler with water from the sink. This he brought to Claire and presented it with a waiter's flourish. She drank it without a word.

He said, "Do you like it?"

"Yes. Very much. It is a pleasant drink."

"Would you like some more?"

"Not now," she said.

He sat beside her on the bed, and kissed her with a clownish sweetness, holding her elbows, and she responded innocently, putting her cool nose against his neck. Then she said, "Wait."

She untied the drawstring at her waist and shook herself out of her dress. She did this quickly, like someone impatient to swim. When she was naked they kissed again, and he was almost alarmed by the way her tongue insisted in his mouth and her foraging hands pulled clumsily at his clothes. Soon after, they made love, and in the darkness, when it had ended, Harper thought he heard her whimper with dissatisfaction.

He woke. She was across the room, speaking French.

"What is it?"

"I am calling a taxi, to go home."

"Don't go," he said. "Besides, I don't think the phone works."

"I have to take my pill."

The phone worked. *I am in Paris:* he said it in a groggy foolish voice.

Claire, who was dressing, said, "Pardon?"

The next day was a repetition of the previous day. He waited at the hotel for Undershaw to ring. At four, he went to the office. This time there were no preliminaries; only romance required them, and this was no romance. Harper was glad of that, and glad too that he was not particularly attracted to Claire. Since his marriage — and he was happy with his wife — he had not been attracted to any other woman. It did not make him calm; indeed, it worried him, because he knew that if he did fall for another woman it would matter and he would have to leave home. They skipped the bar, ate quickly, then hurried to the hotel and went to bed, hardly speaking.

In the pitch dark of early morning, he waited for her to make her telephone call. But she was asleep. He woke her. She was startled, then seemed to remember where she was. He said, "Don't you have to go?"

She muttered rapidly in French, then came fully awake and said, "I brought my pill."

Harper slept badly; Claire emitted gentle satisfied snores. In the morning she opened her eyes wide and said, "I had a *cauchemar*."

"Really?" The word, which he knew, bewitched him.

She said, "You have a beautiful word in English for *cauchemar*."

"*Cauchemar* is a beautiful word," he said, and quoted,

> How much it means that I say this to you —
> Without these friendships — life, what *cauchemar!*

"I don't understand," she said.

"A poem," said Harper.

She pretended to shudder. She said, "What is *cauchemar* in English?"

"Nightmare."

"So beautiful," she said.

"What was your *cauchemar* about?"

"My — nightmare" — she smiled, savoring the word — "it was about us. You and me. We were in a house together, with a cat. It was quite an ordinary cat, but it was very hungry. I wanted to make love with you. That is my trouble, you see. I am too direct. The cat was in our bedroom."

"Where was this bedroom — Europe?"

"Paris," she said. "The cat was so hungry it was sitting on the floor and crying. We couldn't make love until we had fed it. We gave it some food. But when the cat ate the food it caught fire and burned — oh, it was horrible! Each time it swallowed it burned some more. It did not burn like a cat, but like a human, like Jan Palach. You know Jan Palach?"

Harper did not know the name. He said, "A saint?" — because her tone seemed to describe a martyr.

"No, no, no," said Claire. She was troubled.

Harper said, "It's about being a lesbian — your dream. Killing the cat, us making love."

"Of course," she said. "I have thought of that."

Her troubled look had left her; now she was abstracted, her features stilled by thought.

A fear rose in Harper that he was not in Europe at all, but trapped in a strange place with a sad crazy woman. He had made a great mistake in becoming involved with her. It was worse when they were dressing, for the telephone rang and Harper panicked and screamed, "Don't touch it!" He imagined that it was his wife, and he felt guilty and ashamed to be in this room with this incomprehensible woman. He had never loved his wife more. He seized the phone: Undershaw.

"It's ready. You can come over."

"Thank you," said Harper, tongue-tied with gratitude. He turned to Claire. "I've got to go to the office."

But she was buckling her small watch to her wrist. "Look at the time," she cried. "I'm late!"

They arrived separately — it was his idea — so that no one

would suspect what they had done. Harper, who had spent days wishing to punch Undershaw in the face, introduced himself to the gray, rather tall Englishman feeling no malice at all. He took the parcel of money and locked himself in a small room to count it. He repeated the procedure, and when he was satisfied the amount was correct he packed the money in neat bundles in the briefcase. And, as if he knew how long it took to count eighty-five thousand dollars, Undershaw knocked at the door just as Harper finished.

"If everything's in order I'll be off then," said Undershaw.

"Take care," said Harper, and watched him go.

In the outer office, Claire was filling her handbag. Harper paused, because he believed it was expected of him to ask her out to dinner — he would not be able to leave until the next day.

Claire said, "I can't see you tonight. I am meeting a woman. I may have an adventure. You can stay — shut the door and it will lock."

"I hope she's nice," said Harper. "Your woman."

"Yes," said Claire, ladylike in concentration. She went to the door and stuck out her lower lip. "She is my fiancé's girl friend."

When she had left, Harper wanted to sit down. But the chairs disgusted him. There were four of them in this dreadful yellow room, this rallying place for the crooked — they were not evil, but idle. The room had held Bumgarner, and Claire, and Undershaw; and now they had gone on their tired errands. But their snailtracks were still here. There are rooms — his hotel room was one — in which the weak leave their sour hope behind; from which they set out to succeed at small deceptions and fail in the hugest way. Harper wanted to be home. He felt insulted and had never hated himself more. The briefcase, weighted with money, reminded him that he was still in Paris, and that he would have to complete his own shameful errand before he could look for a new job in the United States of America.

VOLUNTEER SPEAKER

IT ANNOYED ME when people asked, because I had to tell them I had just been in Southeast Asia. That was a deceptively grand name for the small dusty town where I was American consul. But who has heard of Ayer Hitam? Officially, it was a Hardship Post — the designation meant extra money, a Hardship Allowance I could not spend. There was no hardship, but there was boredom, and nothing to buy to relieve me of that. With a free month before I was due in Washington to await reassignment, I decided to finance a private trip to Europe — another grand name. One town on my route was Saarbrücken, where the river formed the French-German border. It looked like magic the day I arrived; at dinner it seemed like a version of the town I had left in Malaysia.

My choice of Saarbrücken was not accidental. The Flints, Charlie and Lois, had been posted here after their stint in Kuala Lumpur. They had been urging me to visit them: the single man and the childless couple are natural allies, in an uncomplicated way. Charlie had accepted this minor post because he had refused to spend the usual two deskbound years in Washington. He had not lived in Washington for fifteen years. It was his boast — no good telling him that Washington had changed — and it meant that he had to keep on the move. A little patience and politicking would have earned him promotions. "Next stop Abu Dhabi," he used to say. That was before Abu Dhabi became important. At dinner, he said, "Next stop Rwanda. I don't even know the capital."

"Kigali," I said. "It's a hole."

"I keep forgetting you're an old Africa hand."

Lois said, "One of these days, the State Department's going to send us to a really squalid place. Then Charlie will have to admit it's worse than Washington."

"I didn't squawk in Medan," said Flint. "I didn't squawk in K.L. I actually liked Bangalore. They once threatened me with Calcutta. The idiots in Washington don't even know that Calcutta morale is the highest in the foreign service. The housing's fantastic and you can get a cook for ten bucks. That's my kind of place. Only squirts want Paris. And the guys on the third floor — they like Paris, too."

"Who are the guys on the third floor?"

"The spooks," said Flint. "That's what they call them here."

Lois winked at me. "He's been squawking here."

"I didn't think anyone complained in Europe," I said.

"This isn't Europe," said Flint. "It's not even Germany. Half the people here pretend they're French."

"I like these border towns," I said. "The ambiguity, the rigmarole at the customs post, the rumors about smugglers — it's a nice word, smugglers. I associate borders with mystery and danger."

"The only danger here is that the ambassador will cable me that he wants to go fishing. Then I have to waste a week fixing up his permits and finding his driver a place to stay. And all the other security — antikidnap measures so he can catch minnows. Jesus, I hate this job."

Flint had turned grouchy. To change the subject, I said, "Lois, this is a wonderful meal."

"You're sweet to say so," Lois said. "I'm taking cooking lessons. Would you believe it?"

"It's a kind of local sausage," said Flint, spearing a tube of encased meat with his fork. "Everything's a kind of local sausage. You'd get arrested for eating this in Malaysia. The wine's drinkable, though. All wine-growing countries are right-wing — ever think of that?"

"Charlie still hasn't forgiven me for not learning to cook," Lois said. She stared at her husband, a rather severe glaze on her eyes that fixed him in silence; but she went on with what seemed calculated lightheartedness, "I can't help the fact that he made me spend my early married life in countries where cooks cost ten dollars a month."

"Consequently, Lois is a superb tennis player," said Flint.

A certain atmosphere was produced by this remark, but it was a passing cloud, a blade of half-dark, no more. It hovered and was gone. Lois rose abruptly and said, "I hope you left room for dessert."

Charlie did not speak until Lois was in the kitchen. I see I have written "Charlie" rather than "Flint"; but he had changed, his tone grew confidential. He said, "I'm very worried about Lois. Ever since we got here she's been behaving funnily. People have mentioned it to me — they're not used to her type. I mean, she cries a lot. She might be heading for a nervous breakdown. You try doing a job with a sick person on your hands. It's a whole nother story. I'm glad you're here — you're good for her."

It was unexpected and it came in a rush, the cataract of American candor. I murmured something about Lois looking perfectly all right to me.

"It's an act — she's a head case," he said. "I don't know what to do about her. But you'd be doing me a big favor if you made allowances. Be good to her. I'd consider it a favor — "

Lois entered the room on those last words. She was carrying a dark heap of chocolate cake. She said, "You don't have to do something just because Charlie asks you to."

"We were talking about the Volunteer Speakers Program,"

said Flint, with unfaltering coolness and even a hint of boredom: it was a masterful piece of acting. "As I was saying, I'm supposed to be lining up speakers, but we haven't had one for months. The last time I was in Bonn, the ambassador put a layer of shit in my ear — what am I doing? I told him — bringing culture to the Germans. The town's a thousand years old. There were Romans here! He didn't think that was very funny. It would help if you gave a talk for me at the Center."

Lois reached across the table and squeezed my hand. There was more reassurance than caution in the gesture. She said, "Pay no attention to him. He could have all the volunteer speakers he wants. He just doesn't ask them."

"Herr Friedrich on Roman spittoons, Gräfin von Spitball on the local aristocracy. That's what Europe's big on — memories. It hasn't got a future, but what a past! There's something decadent about nostalgia — I mean, really diseased."

"Charlie doesn't like Germans," said Lois. "No one likes them. For fifteen years, all I've heard is how inefficient people are in tropical countries. Guess what the big complaint is here? Germans are efficient. They do things on time, they keep their word — this is supposed to be sinister!"

Flint said, "They're machines."

"He used to call Malays 'superslugs,' " said Lois.

"And Germans think we're diseased," said Flint. "They talk about German culture. What's German culture? These days it's American culture — the same books, the same music, the same movies, even the same clothes. They've bought us wholesale, and they have the nerve to sneer." His harangue left him gasping. With a kind of mournful sincerity he said, "I'd consider it a favor if you did a lecture. We have a slot tomorrow — there's a sewing circle that meets on Thursdays."

He was asking me to connive at his deception, and he knew I could not decently refuse him such a simple request. I said, "Doesn't one need a topic?"

"The white man's burden. War stories. Life in the East.

Like the time the locals besieged your consulate and burned the flag."

"All the locals did was smile and drink my whiskey."

"Improvise," he said, twirling his wine glass. "Ideally, I'd like something on 'America's Role in a Changing World' — like, What good is foreign aid? What are the responsibilities of the superpowers? The oil crisis with reference to Islam and the Arab states, Are we at a crossroads? Look, all they want is to hear you speak English. We had to discontinue the language program after the last budget cuts. They'll be glad to see a new face. They're pretty sick of mine."

Lois squeezed my hand again. "Welcome to Europe."

* * *

The next morning, trying sleepily to imagine what I would say in my lecture — and I hated Flint for making me go through with this charade — I was startled by a knock at the door. I sat up in bed. It was Lois.

"I forgot to warn you about breakfast," she said, entering the room. Her tone was cheerfully apologetic, but her movements were bold. At first I thought she was in her pajamas. I put on my glasses and saw she was in a short pleated skirt and a white jersey. The white clothes and their cut gave her a girlish look, and at the same time contradicted it, exaggerating her briskness. Tennis had obviously kept her in shape. She was in her early forties — younger than Charlie — but was trim and hard-fleshed. She had borne no children — it was childbirth that left the marks of age on a woman's body. She had a flat stomach, a server's stride, and as she approached the bed I noticed the play of muscles in her thighs. She was an odd apparition, but a woman in a tennis outfit looks too athletic in a businesslike way to be seductive.

She was still talking about breakfast, not looking at me, but pacing the floor at the foot of the bed. Charlie didn't normally have more than a coffee, she said. There was grapefruit in the fridge and cereal on the sideboard. The coffee was made. Did I want eggs?

"I'll have a coffee with Charlie," I said.

"He's gone. He left the house an hour ago."

"Don't worry about me. I can look after myself."

Lois's tennis shoes squeaked as she paced the polished floor. Then she stopped and faced me. "I'm worried about Charlie," she said. "I suppose you thought he was joking last night about the ambassador. It's serious — he hasn't accomplished anything here. Everyone knows it. And he doesn't care."

Almost precisely the words he had used about her: I wondered whether they were playing a game with me.

"I'm his volunteer speaker," I said. "That's quite a feather in his cap."

"You don't think so, but it is. He's in real trouble. He told the ambassador he was thinking of taking early retirement."

"Might not be a bad idea," I said.

"He said, 'I can always sell second-hand cars. I've been selling second-hand junk my whole foreign service career.' That's what he told the ambassador! I was flabbergasted. Then he told me it was a joke. It was at a staff meeting — all the PAOs were there. But no one laughed. I don't blame them — it's not funny."

I wanted to get out of bed. I saw that this would not be simple while she was in the room. I could not think straight, sitting up, with the blankets across my lap, my hair in my eyes.

Lois said, "Can I get in?"

I have always felt that if a person wants something very badly, and if it is not unreasonable, he should have it, no matter what. I usually feel like supplying it myself. Once, I gave my hunting knife to a Malay. He admired it; he wanted it; he had some use for it. Generosity is easy to justify. I always lose what I don't need.

I considered Lois's question and then said, "Yes — sure," convinced that Charlie had not misled me: something was wrong with her.

She got in quickly, without embarrassment. She said, "He's mentally screwed up, he really is."

"Poor Charlie."

We lay under the covers, side by side, like two Boy Scouts in a big sleeping bag, sheltering from the elements in clumsy comradeship. Lois had not taken off her tennis shoes: I could feel the canvas and rubber against my shins. Her shoes seemed proof that Charlie had not exaggerated her mental state.

"He thinks it's funny. It's me who's suffering. People pity mental cases — it's their families they should pity."

"That's pitching it a bit strongly, isn't it?" I tried to shift my hand from the crisp pleats of her skirt. "Charlie may be under a little strain, but he hardly qualifies as a mental case."

"A month ago we're at a party. It was endless — one of these German affairs. They really love their food, and their idea of fun is to get stinking drunk and sing loud. There's no social stigma attached to drunkenness here. So everyone was laughing stupidly and the men were behaving like jackasses. One of them took my shawl and put it over his head and did a Wagner bit. And there was this Italian — just a hanger-on, he wasn't a diplomat. He suggested they all go to a restaurant. It's two in the morning, everyone's eaten, and he wants to go to a restaurant! There was a sort of general move to the door — they're all yelling and laughing. I said to Charlie, 'Count me out — I'm tired.'

" 'You never want to do anything,' he said.

"I told him he could go if he wanted to. He gave me the car keys and I went home alone. I was asleep when he came back. There was a big commotion at the front door — it was about five. I go to the door and who do I see? Charlie. And the Italian. They're holding hands."

I almost laughed. But Lois was on the verge of tears. I felt her body stiffen.

"It was awful. The Italian had this guilty, sneaky look on his face, as if he'd been caught in the act. I saw that he wanted to drop the whole thing. He wouldn't look at me. Charlie was gray — absolutely gray. He wasn't even drunk — he looked sick, crazy, and he kept holding this Italian by the hand. He told me to go back to bed.

" 'I'm not going back to bed until he leaves,' I said.

" 'This is my friend,' he said. His friend! They're holding hands! He dragged the Italian into the house and I really wanted to hit both of them. Charlie said, 'We're staying.'

" 'Not him,' I said. 'He's not staying in my house.'

" 'You never let me have any friends,' said Charlie, and he starts staggering around with this other guy. I thought I was dreaming, it was so ridiculous.

" 'I don't care what you do,' I said, 'but you're not taking this creep into my house.' Then I got hysterical, I started screaming, I hardly knew what I was saying.

"Charlie said, 'All right, then, let's go.' And off they went, hand in hand, out the door. I don't know where they went. I didn't see Charlie until that night. He looked terrible — I don't even think he'd been to work. He hasn't mentioned it since. And you deny he's a mental case."

Listening to her story, it struck me that I hardly knew Charlie Flint. He was as frenzied as anyone in the embassy, and he had a theory that the embassy wives were going to start an insurrection, but our relationship was mainly professional. I knew nothing of his personal life beyond the fact that he drank too much; that fact applied to everyone I met in the foreign service. I regarded his determination to stay out of Washington as a worthy aim. He wasn't ambitious. And he had prepared me for his wife's oddness.

I replied to her in platitudes: Don't jump to conclusions, things will settle down, and so forth. What else could I offer? I did not know her well, and I was in bed with her. I said, as an afterthought, "You're not suggesting he's gay, are you?"

"Do you think I'd care about that?" she said. "You've been in the bush for two years, so you don't know. But being bisexual is the big thing in Europe these days. Everyone's gay.

The men think it's fashionable, almost masculine — proof that you don't have any hang-ups. They're always hugging each other, holding hands — God only knows what else they do, though I have a pretty good idea. I'm telling you, Europe makes Southeast Asia look civilized. I get propositioned about once a week — by women!"

"Are you tempted?"

"No," Lois said, "I tried it."

"With a woman?"

She nodded; her whole body moved, and she wore a curious half-smile. "A German chick. About nineteen. Very pretty. It didn't work out." She made a face. "Charlie wanted me to. That's why I didn't take it seriously. I thought it would encourage him in his craziness. Now, when I think about it, I just laugh." She shifted sideways on the bed, propped herself up on one arm and said, "How come you're so normal?"

"Everything is human."

"You're making excuses for Charlie."

"Charlie has a conscience."

"Don't you?"

"I don't know. But I know that the lack of it can make some people look fairly serene, even harmless and normal. Charlie hasn't hurt anyone."

"He's hurt me!" Lois cried, and I felt her shoe. "I'm sorry," she said. "I didn't mean to kick you. But what good is it saying, 'Everything's human and everything's normal'? We were in Indonesia, India, Malaysia — yes, things were normal in those places. But Europe's different. And I'm telling you, I can't handle it."

I felt sure she was mistaken, but I didn't want to contradict her, since she appeared to take everything as a personal attack. She saw Charlie's drunken hand-holding as an affront to her, but this casual mention of *a German chick* — wasn't that equally odd? She didn't appear to think so. I understood why she was lying to me, though it was not in character for her to belittle Charlie. Adultery is a great occasion for lying; the wife in another man's bed usually talks about her husband.

I said, "I'm glad I came to Europe. I had no idea it was so lively. It makes Ayer Hitam seem rather tame."

"Where are you going after this?"

"Up the Rhine. I'm leaving tonight, after my talk. I'll be in Düsseldorf for a few days."

"Are you staying with Murray Goldsack?"

"Charlie gave me his name. But I'll probably stay in a hotel."

"Charlie gave you his name," Lois said bitterly. "He would. We were up there three weeks ago. Another disaster."

I didn't want to hear it, but she had already begun.

"The Goldsacks have been there about a year. She writes poetry, he's big on painting — he'll show you the gallery he opened. It's full of pretentious crap — stupid, simple, neurotic blurs. Doesn't anyone paint people anymore? The Goldsacks don't have any children. In fact, when they got married they signed a contract saying they wouldn't have any kids and deciding who'd get what when they split up. They assumed they'd split up eventually — Murray will give you all the statistics. They're very modern laid-back people with a house full of crap art and heads full of crap opinions. Over dinner, they told us how they keep their marriage alive.

"Get this. They play games. Like 'White Night.' Sue puts on a white dress, white slippers, white everything. Then she cooks a white meal — mashed potatoes, steamed fish, cauliflower, chablis. Murray wears a white suit. Then they get drunk and go to it."

"That doesn't sound so odd," I said. She was not lying, but repeating a lie.

"They also have Black Night, Red Night. Or Indian Night. She puts on a sari, cooks a curry, they burn incense and run through the *Kamasutra*."

"Tell me about Eskimo Night. Do they rub noses?"

"Be serious, will you? Murray was telling me about it — we

were in his living room. As he was describing these dressing-up games I noticed he was filling my glass. This little squirt was trying to get me drunk! I was feeling pretty rotten, and he was annoyed that I wasn't drinking fast enough. So he pulled out some pot and rolled me a joint. I once tried some in K.L., but it wasn't anything like this. My brain turned into oatmeal. Then I looked around and didn't see Charlie. I was panicky. 'Where's Charlie?' I said. Murray looked at me. 'Oh, he's with Sue.'

" 'Where are they?' I said.

"He pointed to a door — the door was closed. I said, 'I've got to talk to him' — I don't know why I said it. Maybe it was that stuff I had just smoked.

"Murray said, 'Don't go in there. They don't want you to.'

" 'How do you know what they want?' I said. He sort of chuckled. I said, 'Hey, what's going on?'

"He had a really evil look on his face. He said, 'You really want to know?'

"Then I knew. I wanted to cry. I said, 'My husband's in that room with your wife!' He said something like, 'So what?' and put his arm around me. I pushed him away and stood up. He got mad at me — he was really peeved. He tried to grab me again, and I hit him. He said, 'Hey, what's wrong with you?'

"What's wrong with *me?* This man's a cultural affairs officer in the United States embassy. He's supposed to be a diplomat, he gives lectures, he makes statements to the press, he writes reports — or whatever they do. And he's peeved because I won't cooperate with his wife-swapping! It was too much. After an hour or so, Charlie and Sue came out looking pretty pale and pushing their clothes back in place. We all had a drink and talked about — Jesus, we talked about Jimmy Carter and the budget cuts. The next day we left. Charlie wouldn't talk about the other thing — the monkey business."

Lois was silent for a while. Then she turned over onto her side, her back to me. I got up on one elbow and, seeing that she was crying, I put my arm around her to comfort her.

She said, "Hold me tight — please." I did. She murmured, "That's nice."

What now? I thought.

She said, "Charlie never pays any attention to me."

"I can't help liking him," I said.

Lois said, "I'm married to him," and then, "Don't let go."

"I feel a bit silly," I said. "Should we be doing this?"

"I get nothing," she said. "Nothing, nothing. This isn't a life."

"You're going to miss your tennis."

She twisted away from me and heaved her legs up.

"What are you doing, Lois?"

"Getting these damn shoes off."

I said, "I'm supposed to be having lunch with Charlie. I couldn't face him. Please don't take your shoes off."

"He doesn't care," she said.

Another lie: for all his frenzy and occasional deceit, there was no man who would have cared more about his wife's infidelity. Remember, they had no children to encumber their intimacy, so they were like children themselves — such couples so often are.

"That seems worse," I said, resenting her ineptness.

She pressed her back against me, moving her skirt sinuously on my thighs; and still facing away she uttered a despairing groan.

"Then just hold me," she said. "I'll be all right in a minute."

When she got out of bed her pleated skirt was crushed and her socks had slipped down. She brushed herself off, adjusted her socks, and tucked in her jersey. She looked as if she had just played her match and been defeated.

She said, "I feel very virtuous."

"I don't," I said. Then she was out the door. I thought: *She is insane.*

* * *

Charlie was late for lunch. When he arrived, I looked for indications of the craziness Lois had attributed to him. But there were none. She needed to believe he was crazy, in order to make excuses for herself.

He said, "Do you really have to go to Düsseldorf after the lecture?"

"The lecture was your idea," I said. "If it wasn't for that I'd be on the train now."

"You're welcome to stay as long as you like. Lois was hoping you would."

I said, "I don't think there's much I can do for her."

"Fair enough." He seemed gloomy and almost apologetic, as if he had guessed at what had gone on that morning between Lois and me. I did not want to upset him further by telling him her wild stories. He said, "I'd leave this place tomorrow except for one thing. This is the first place Lois can live a normal life. I'm staying for her sake. Believe me, it's a sacrifice. But there are good doctors here. The best medical care. That's what she needs."

"I understand." I could not say more without revealing that I pitied him.

"You'll like Düsseldorf. Goldsack's a live wire. A very bright guy — he's got a big future in the foreign service. He'll make ambassador as sure as anything. His wife's fun, and I think I should tell you — she's an easy lay."

That was the first clue I had that Lois might not have been completely wrong about Charlie. And it made me all the more eager to meet the Goldsacks. I left immediately after my lecture, and two days later was in Murray Goldsack's office.

"Flint cabled me that you were coming," he said. "I've been looking over your bio. It's really impressive." Goldsack was small and dark, in his early thirties, and he looked me over closely, giving me the strong impression that I was being interviewed and appraised. He said, "I wish I had your Southeast Asia experience. My wife keeps saying we should put in for a tour there."

"You might be disappointed."

"I'm never bored," he said, and made it sound like a reproach. "Flint said you might be available as a volunteer speaker."

"Other people do it so much better," I said.

"Give us a chance to entertain you at least," he said. "We'd like to have you and your wife over for a meal. I hope you'll both be able to make it."

"If my bio says I'm married, you've been misinformed."

Goldsack laughed. "What I mean is, I'd rather you didn't come alone."

I said, "I know an antique dealer in town. He's a lovely fellow. Now, he's someone you might like to consider as a volunteer speaker."

"Wonderful," said Goldsack. He jumped up and shook my hand to signal the meeting was over. "I'll leave a message at your hotel with the details."

That was the last I saw of Goldsack. There was no message, which was just as well, because there was no antique dealer. I thought: *Poor Lois.*

THE GREENEST ISLAND

1

THEY HAD CHOSEN San Juan because it was cheap that year and it was as far away as they could get from people who knew they were not married. They guessed they would be found out eventually, but to be caught at home, mimicking marriage, playing house — that was dangerous. They were in trouble and ashamed of it, but being young felt the shame as an undeserved insult. They had discovered this island like castaways in a children's story, who stumble ashore and learn to live among the surprises of a tropical place. The footprints of cannibals, bright birds, coconut palms!

But in 1961 Puerto Rico was a poor ruined island. There was no romance — they had brought none. It was green, that was all; and though the green was overstated, there was a kind of yellow delay lurking in the color. They were unprepared and a little frightened. They had nothing but their pretense of audacity and three hundred and twenty dollars. No return tickets: they had no particular plans. The hotel was dirty and expensive — they couldn't live there. By chance, they found a furnished room on the Calle de San Francisco. It was only a room, but here they felt safe enough to write to their families and tell them what they had done.

Paula had hidden her pregnancy from her parents. She had planned to tell them, but for four months she had lived with Duval in his college town — another shabby room. She wrote home then; she told them she was in New York, working. I need a year off, she said. Her parents understood. There were two other couples in that house — newly married students, with stingy interests, busy with their studies, wanting privacy in their nests of notebooks and term papers. Noisy and hilarious in their rooms, outside they were incurious. Duval saw them on the stairs and couldn't match the nighttime laughter to their grave daylit faces. When the spring semester ended, Paula had said, "I can't go home — they'd kill me," and Duval had agreed to do something.

He was nineteen, impatient to be older and with a sense that he was incomplete. He read; his imagination blazed; he tried to write. Although he had accomplished little he had the conviction that he was marked for some great windfall, without sacrifice. He believed in his luck, and this belief made him unassailable but solitary and secretive. He could do whatever he chose to; he was confident of his ability to write humorously and well. His spark warmed him like a star and promised that success would come to him with age, in a matter of years. He was certain of it, but that was before Paula had shrunk this future he imagined. Her news had brought the future to his feet, unexpectedly freezing him. He was no longer alone. She was twenty-one, a woman, and she resented the difference in their ages, though she looked younger than he with her sly pretty face and straight blonde-streaked hair and warm skin. He had loved her.

A year before he might have married her. But he had stopped loving her, the fever left him, and a month later she had said he'd made her pregnant. It happened so fast there wasn't time to talk about their feelings, and Duval didn't want to hurt her more by saying he didn't love her. Love didn't matter now. The fact was greater: she was going to have his baby. For a confused month when they were apart, in letters, they had argued about the alternatives. The thought of an abortion frightened her. "Knitting needles," she said. He calmed her and telephoned a woman in Somerville. The woman said she would do it for sixty dollars and that he should call back. He did, a week later. The woman was hysterical; she screamed, she cried. She would be arrested, she said in a terrible voice. But she agreed to do it. "It's the last time!" Duval never called her again. And it was too late to get married, because now they knew what their marriage would be: a temporary urgency, a trap, the end of their lives. They wanted more than that and they knew they were not in love.

Still, they were afraid; but less afraid when they were together. They would stay together and hope and try to be kind. They had no choice. And yet they wished to believe that some miracle would release them, that they would wake up free one morning. The wish made them restless and it convinced them that if Paula weren't pregnant, if there were no child, they would not be together.

It seemed necessary to flee and hide. Their parents had begun to wonder about them. Duval said he was going to work on a ship; Paula wrote that she was spending the summer in New York. And when their parents were satisfied with these explanations they flew to San Juan. It was like a further possibility of hope: such a great distance to such a strange place; the humid heat, the smells, yellow-brown faces, the sight of palms. The miracle might happen here, on this green island. They waited in their room.

In the morning from their window they could see the high stucco houses of the old city with their clifflike balconies, and the ramparts of the fort and the jutting roofs of the settlement that was pitched between the sea wall and the ocean, the stick and palm leaf slum known locally as *La Perla*, the pearl. There was music, one song played over and over, yakking trumpets, the snap of guitars and sad Spanish tenors. There were cries from the street: the paper seller calling out " — *parcial*," the chattering of the boy beggars, the ice-cream man with his cart of *piraguas;* and the frantic din of an old woman yelling in Spanish. They heard her for days — she sounded hurt — and then, when they saw her, she was doing nothing more alarming than selling lottery tickets in front of the Colorama Toy Store. She had to scream. Her competitor was a dwarf with tiny legs and an enormous head, who sat in a chair in the Plaza Colon, just around the corner. He looked at first glance like a severed head propped on a chair seat, and most people bought their tickets from him, for charity, for luck.

Duval explored the neighborhood and brought back stories. The people were damaged and crazy, or else very sad. There were homeless boys and old women who slept on the marble benches in the plaza, under the statue of Columbus. The paper seller — his face burned black, his hair burned orange — stood in the sun all day, and at night got drunk and wept hoarsely and shook his penis at passers-by. There was a one-legged man who wore a red scarf on his head and when he paused to beg hooked his stump over the bar of his crutch and glared like a pirate and demanded money. There was a legless man who rode up and down the Calle de San Francisco in a low clattering cart, pulling himself along with his hands. One morning Duval saw a group of excited men being harangued by a soldier. "They are starting an army," said an onlooker. "They will invade Santo Domingo and kill Trujillo."

It rained each afternoon, sometimes for a few minutes, occasionally for twenty minutes or more. It was loud; it crackled like burning sticks and drove people into doorways — the crazy ones, the five-dollar whores from La Gloria, the beggars, schoolgirls, amputees, the recruits for the invading army — and there they waited, watching the rain, not speaking. After the rain the buildings dripped and there would be a hot hideous smell in the air of wet garbage and yellow sunlit vapor rising from the street. There were few tourists — it wasn't the season. There were sailors from the navy base and merchant seamen who crowded in from the docks and lingered in the plaza where there were whores and shade and cigar stalls.

It looked dangerous — an island of fugitives, temporary people and harmed hopeless souls. Paula and Duval felt they belonged there: such strangeness could make them anonymous. But they were scared, too — worried they'd be robbed, uncertain about the future, so far. Duval went out alone during the day, and at night, when the old city was those harsh voices and songs and the sound of traffic and the roar of the sea near La Perla, he stayed in with Paula. At midnight all the radios in the district played the national anthem: *La tierra di Borinquén, donde me nacido. Isla de flores* — Duval knew the words, but not their meaning.

Their room faced the street. There were two other rooms on that floor, Mr. Ruiz's and Antonio's. Mr. Ruiz lived in Arecibo. He went home to his family at weekends and on Sunday night returned alone to his room, bringing a bag of mangoes. He said he hated his room. He said, "It can get very bad here." He hated the ants, the cockroaches, the darkness. "I burn the ants," he said, and then, "I like to hear the little snaps when they die."

Antonio disliked Mr. Ruiz; Antonio wanted Puerto Rico to be the fifty-first state, Mr. Ruiz wanted independence. When he saw Paula and Duval Antonio always called out, "State fifty-one!" Antonio worked at night — he never said where. In the afternoon he stood in the doorway on Calle de San Francisco muttering each time a woman went past: *"Fea . . . fea,"* ugly, ugly. He said he did it to engage them, and sometimes they stopped and talked and went upstairs with him. He lived in the next room and those times his elbows knocked on the wall and his bed creaked as if it were being sawed in half.

The building was owned by Señora Gonzales, a young plump widow who dressed heavily in black. Her curio shop was on the ground floor, and all afternoon she made souvenirs out of coconut fiber and bamboo, place mats and dolls with witches' faces. She was uncritical without being friendly. She had rented Paula and Duval the room and had asked no questions. She had sized them up swiftly and appeared to know they had run away.

They began going out together, always choosing the same route: down to the plaza, over to the fort, up the hill to the cathedral where Ponce de León was buried, and then meeting their own street at the top end, at Baldorioty de Castro. They spoke to no one; the language was incomprehensible. They bought food by pointing and smiling and showing their money: a child's effort, a child's gestures. Each day they had the same meal: mushroom soup thickened with rice, pineapple, ice cream; Paula drank a quart of milk. They kept a record of their expenses and saw their money trickling away. Dreadful; it was what they expected. This green disfigured place was the world. It was hot during the day and at night it stank. There were cripples everywhere. But they had sought it, and they deserved to be here. It matched their own punished mood. And sometimes they felt lucky to be surviving it. No one here could accuse them of betraying their parents. They were what they seemed, a young couple expecting a baby, anonymous in the tropical crowd.

They seldom quarreled. Although they felt they hadn't the right to be happy, they experienced a tentative enjoyment, a little freedom alone in this restricted place. Their occasional anger they made into silence. Paula decided to study Spanish, Duval to write — soon, to use the time.

Alone; but they were not alone. Both sensed it. There was someone else who crouched darkly between them. They dwelled in the present and moved forward only by time's slow fractions. They did not speak of the future because they would not mention the baby. They avoided all talk of that — the choice it demanded, the rush of time it implied. It was more than a weight: it was a human presence. They spent their evenings talking without consequence of the oddities they saw — the religious processions, the green lizards on the back roof, the amputee in his noisy cart: the sunlight removed the cheating blur of nightmarishness and made each sight a vivid spectacle.

They were aware of their omission. It was as if there were a third person with them, sentient but mute, to whom they could not refer without risking misunderstanding or offense. It was someone they did not know, as mysterious to them as anyone on the island, and contained by Paula — when she came close to whisper she bumped Duval with the stranger. And so their evenings had sudden silences and were usually stilled by the sense of a small helpless listener. They were like people sitting in a room to wait for a signal from that third person, and there was about their gentleness a fearful timidity of waiting that was as solemn as a deathwatch.

Others reminded them of why they were waiting. Mr. Ruiz, who gave them mangoes, brought out pictures of his children and named them: Angel, Maria, José, Pablo, Costanza. His wife, he said, was also pregnant: he nudged Duval, trying to share the pride and resignation of fatherhood. Antonio was respectful, and when he saw Duval alone in La Gloria he asked, "How is she?" as if Paula were ill and Duval needed reassurance. Paula remained healthy, though she complained of the humidity and said walking made her feet swell. So each afternoon she lay down and rested. One day, two weeks after their arrival on the island, she said her ankles felt huge. Duval massaged them and said, "Does that hurt?" She said no. He pressed harder; she didn't react. He said, "You're all right," but several minutes later he looked again at the ankle and saw the deep dent of his thumbprint.

The heat drugged them. They went to bed when they heard the national anthem and did not wake until the traffic and street noise racketed against the shutters. She slept soundly, perspiring, a film of heat on her skin; but just before she dropped off to sleep she thought how cruel it all was. Anyone else would have been happy, expectant, making preparations. She was doubtful and afraid. She wanted something else; she was too young to give in to this. A life she did not want was being forced upon her.

Duval's sleep was shallow, disturbed by the last thing he did before he went to bed. This was his journal. Not a diary — he never mentioned the progress of the pregnancy; he wrote undated paragraphs about what he saw on the island. It was, he knew, the sort of book a castaway might keep, a record of wonders and surprises: the beggars, the difficult heat, the ants, the lizards. He did not write about himself. He wanted to survive, and he still believed in his luck. He went to bed; he remembered; he woke up and dreaded to inquire where he was or why. He felt he was performing a service, obediently, unwillingly, without love — as if he had been assigned this protective task for a certain period. When it was over he would be free. But he worried. He had already been away too long; he would not be able completely to re-enter that former self. This task, this place, was undoing him, and he feared that having been forced this far he might never go back.

The silence was broken one night by Paula's crying. He tried to comfort her. He said it was hot — he would open a shutter.

"No," she said. She hadn't moved. She lay on her side, facing away from him. In a small clear voice she said, "What are we going to do?"

2

IT WAS A HOLIDAY on the island, Muñoz Rivera's birthday. They had no idea who he was, but the plaza was festive, jammed with buses and taxis and decorated with banners showing Muñoz Rivera's big pink *hidalgo* face. The dark mob, sweating with gaiety, surged beneath the blowing portraits.

The shops were closed, there were no newspapers, and even the girls from La Gloria were taking the day off. Duval saw six of them piling into a taxi with towels and baskets of food — off to the beach. Family groups — the scowling fathers walking a little apart — paraded in new clothes up the Calle de San Francisco, on their way to the cathedral.

The activity, the noise, stirred Duval, who was watching it all from the window. He said, "Let's go to the beach."

"How much money do we have?" Paula smoothed her blouse over her stomach to emphasize the bulge; she was still small.

"Three dollars." But it was less. He knew the exact amount. He hated himself for keeping track.

"The banks are closed today. We'll have to bring sand-wiches."

"We don't need money."

She said, "You look like a jack-o'-lantern. I hate your face sometimes."

He looked away. The music outside jumped to the window, the same song; and now he could make out the words, *el pesca-dor* and *corazón*, a mournful blaring, continuously repeated.

She said, "I need a shower."

The shower was in a cement hut on the back roof, where clumsy pigeons sometimes fluttered and nested. Paula took her towel and left, but she returned to the room moments later.

"Cockroaches," she said, and threw down the towel. It was a command.

Duval went to the shower and at first saw none. The room was hot and damp, the toilet stank. A sign next to the toilet was lettered in simple Spanish, DO NOT THROW YOUR PAPER ON THE FLOOR. There was an old obscene picture scratched on the wall, with a one-word caption, *chupo*. A cockroach scuttled across the floor and vanished through a crack — gone before he could step on it. There was movement in the sink. He turned on the faucet and toppled the hurrying thing into the plug-hole and kept the water running to drown it. Then he pushed the plastic shower curtain aside. Two reddish blobs slid scratchily down and began working their legs. Duval pulled off a sandal and slapped at them with the sole; there was one more from the tub, several appeared from behind the sink, and the last climbed from the plug-hole twitching water droplets in its jaws. When he was done Duval had killed nine of them. They were dark and scablike and some flew in an ugly burring way, falling crookedly through the air.

Paula took her shower. Duval gathered the Pepsi-Cola bottles that had accumulated under the bed and returned them at La Gloria for the deposit money. Antonio was there on a stool, hunched over a tumbler of brown rum. Seeing Duval, he spoke.

"You want a nice beach?" Antonio licked at his mustache. "Go to Luquillo."

Duval was mystified; then he remembered the thin wall on which he heard Antonio's elbows. He said, "How do I get there?"

"Take a bus to Rio Piedras, then a *público*." Antonio smiled. "Puerto Rico — you like?"

"It's okay," said Duval.

"Too hot. New York's better," said Antonio. "I was there. *Mira,* I got a kid too, in New York. But I come back here. You can play with the girls, but your mother's forever."

Duval said, "Who is Muñoz Rivera?"

"George Washington," said Antonio. "Have a drink. Luis, *venga!*"

"Some other time." Duval gave the empty bottles to the barman and bought two Pepsis and a greasy *frijole* with the money.

Antonio said, "Everybody in New York knows me. Ask them."

Paula was making the sandwiches when he returned to the room. She had hard boiled three eggs and was chopping them on a plate. The bread was stiff and there were tiny dots of white mold on the crusts. She scraped the bread, then wiped it with watery mayonnaise. She said, "We need a refrigerator."

"Those sandwiches will be all right."

"No," she said. "There are ants in the cheese."

Duval took the small brick of cheese and started picking them off. Paula looked disgustedly at him. He wrapped the cheese and dropped it into the wastebasket.

"I was going to throw it away."

"You were going to eat it," she said.

He shook his head. But she was right. The insects no longer bothered him. He believed he had overcome his repugnance. The island was crawling with ants, spiders, cockroaches; during the day there were flies, at night mosquitoes. He brushed them aside; there were too many to kill.

Paula said, "I don't want to go to the beach."

"There's nothing else to do."

They had been to the beach nearby, the one across the road from the Carnegie Library. It lay below a sandy cliff and was rocky and strewn with driftwood and lengths of greasy rope. They had been watched the whole time by prowling children in rags from the shacks of La Perla. They decided to take Antonio's advice and go to Luquillo Beach: Luquillo was famous — it appeared on the travel posters.

It was a long trip, by bus and public taxi, taking them past marshland slums on spindly stilts, high thick canefields broken by fields of young spiky pineapples, and, in the distance, hills as blue and solid as volcanoes. They arrived at the beach at noon and were surprised to find it beautiful and nearly empty. There were groups of picnickers and there was a yellow school bus parked on an apron of broken cement, but there were few people swimming and there was no one lying in the sun.

The beach was white, a crescent of glare shimmering beside a gentle wash of surf in a green bay. The beach itself was not wide; it was entirely fringed by slender palms, and the long fronds swayed like heavy green feathers, making the dry rustling of many kites tumbling in a crosswind, a sound that rose to a hectic flap when the wind strengthened and finally stifled it to a moan. Among the palms children were playing hide and seek; they were quick stripes of light as they ran from trunk to trunk, and their laughter carried through the trees.

Duval and Paula walked down the beach until the schoolchildren were tiny and inaudible. They spread out their towels and lay under a palm and watched the green sea mirror wrinkle in the breeze and flash spangles at them.

"Jake!" She snatched his arm. He looked over and saw in the sand, three feet from her, a dead rat. At her second cry it appeared to move, but that was the lizards, four of them, dark green, darting away at her voice and giving the shriveled carcass movement.

"It's horrible," she said. "Let's go somewhere else."

The lizards raised and lowered their tiny dragon heads and flicked out their tongues. They crept back and resumed feeding on the rat. Paula and Duval had remained motionless, and now they could smell it and hear the flies.

"Wait," said Duval. He got up and, putting the lizards to flight, scooped sand over it until there was only a mound where the stinking thing had been. He smiled at Paula. "Now let's eat."

The sandwiches tasted dustily of decay, the *frijole* was clammy and almost inedible, but they ate without a word. They listened to the rustle of the palms and watched the surf running and curling against the beach. They kept silent; they were new; it was unlucky to complain so soon. A complaint was an admission of weakness, a tactless challenge to the other's strength. Secretly, they wished for rescue — to be delivered from this mock marriage and the certainty of the child. And they craved protection. They were waiting for everything to change, and yet nothing had changed. The sky was unbroken, the sun bore down on the sand, there was no ship in the sea.

Paula had stopped worrying aloud, and Duval admired that in her, but still his affection was tinged with resentment. She had tricked him. He said nothing about that. He knew she felt the same. They were matched in anger.

But her stubborn calm was disturbed by occasional fears. The closest was that Duval would simply leave her — too soon; that she would come back to the room and find him gone. It checked her temper, this fear of desertion: she must not upset him. And he could go easily — he was so young. He got up and walked along the beach a little way, and she saw him as a stranger. It surprised her again to see how skinny he was, in his wrinkled shorts and flapping shirt, faded already, and kicking at the sand, then looking up and making a face at the palm: just a boy, an unreliable boy, who had fooled her.

Duval continued to look at the palm. He stood at the base of the trunk and high up the fronds formed the spokes of a perfect green wheel, at the hub of which was a cluster of shining coconuts. A tropical beach; the sun on the sea; coconuts. It was what he expected from the island: the castaway's vision of survival in the tropical trees. The breeze stirred the palm. Duval took a stone and threw it hard. He missed and tried again and this time hit a coconut. He saw the large thing nod on the fiber that held it.

Paula watched him with increasing irritation. He was so happy, mindlessly pitching stones at the tree. What was wrong with him? He was determined to play. She would have allowed it in a man, but a man didn't behave that way, and this mood in Duval made her feel insecure. She wanted him beside her, attentive, reassuring, and she called out, as she might have to a child, "Stop that!"

Duval paused and shrugged and threw another stone.

"Stop!"

He said, "I want that coconut." He wanted the little victory, the prize. He would get the husk open somehow and offer her the sweet water to drink. And they could eat the white flesh; it would taste better than her sandwiches.

The coconut wouldn't come down. He had hit it squarely but the stones bounced off without dislodging it. He took a heavy stick and threw it and hit it again. The coconut moved slightly, but did not fall. He tried shaking the tree; it did no good. It was such a simple thing, but he could not do it. He threw another stick. This one crashed through the fronds and landed near Paula.

She scrambled to her feet and said, "You almost hit me!"

"Sorry."

"I told you to stop," she said. "Now cut it out."

He left it, and he was annoyed when he returned to her and she looked straight ahead, at the sea. He felt she was mocking him, not because he had tried to knock down the coconut but because he had failed to do it.

She wandered down the beach to the water's edge and holding her skirt against her thighs waded in the shallow surf. Duval looked around; in the distance there were children, and two priests in dark cassocks, brown and yellow stripes between the palm trunks. He slipped off his shorts and put on his bathing suit.

"It's beautiful," he said, coming behind her.

"I wish we could enjoy it." She had said that of the explosive sunsets over the cracked Fortaleza; of the cool plaza; of the gaiety at dusk on the Calle de San Francisco. It was her repetition of it that he hated. That was marriage: repetition.

He strode past her and dived into the water, and was buoyed by its brightness and warmth. It took away his irritation. He swam easily down to the sunlit sea floor, yellow, then blue and green flaked, and he faced depths of purple measured by shafts of light, and flimsy weed stalks trailing up from great smooth boulders. In this colored warmth he experienced a brief sensation of freedom: he was leaving everything behind. He saw his future this way, the happiness he had no words for: success, triumph in a casually chosen place. He moved with weightless ease and it was as if he were breathing underwater, his lungs working without effort. Then a ribbon of cold water passed down his body and he turned and circled back to the hot shallows. He threw his head out of the water, and at the shock of air, the dazzle of bright sun, he gasped.

"You soaked me!" Paula was standing at the shoreline, holding out her sprinkled skirt, exaggerating her distress. "When you dived in you got me all wet. Grow up!"

"It'll dry," he said, and he went close to her.

"Don't drip on me," she said.

"Come in — it's fantastic."

"I don't have a bathing suit." She had tried to find a maternity bathing suit. There were none in the cheap stores: Puerto Rican women didn't swim when they were pregnant. And at the tourists' swim shop at the Hilton they were too expensive.

"You don't need one," he said. "No one's looking." He went into the water again and pulled off his swimming trunks and threw them on the sand.

"No," she said, but she looked around uncertainly. It was the hottest part of the day. The beach was empty, there were no people visible among the trees — the children and the priests had gone; so had the school bus. She was alone and felt tiny and misshapen beside the enormous flat sea. She lifted her skirt, walked a few steps into the water and at once wanted to swim.

She went to the beach, and keeping herself low on the dry sand removed her clothes and folded them, making a neat pile. She entered the water. Instantly, all the heat and heaviness she had felt left her. She had swum out of that clumsy body and into her younger one. She was innocent again. The green sea wrapped her and made her feel small and cool.

They swam apart and spent a long time floating — lying

back and letting the sun burn their faces, their ears stopped by the water's hum. Duval swam over and embraced her. She hugged him and he was aroused.

"Stop," she said, feeling him against her. She turned to face the beach. "Not here."

He barely heard her. He slid between her legs, and they crouched, up to their shoulders in the water. His face was hot and he could see a dusting of salt on her cheeks and the sparkle of water drops on the ringlets of hair at her ears. She looked tense, and she bit her lip as he moved inside her. Their shoulders splashed, touched, parted, and splashed again in the swelling water, and they watched each other almost in embarrassment, hearing the gurgle their bodies made. Then he moved rapidly and stiffened and his face went cold. She looked bewildered, on the point of speaking. He kissed her. The water was quite still and near his arm a little strand of scum floated like a lifeless creature from the deep.

After that they gathered their clothes and rested in the shade. Paula was sleeping lightly on her side, pillowing her head on her arm. Duval left her and walked through the palms to where they opened into rough low bush and stocky trees with thin yellow leaves. Beyond this, miles inland, he saw the dense rain forest he had seen from the *público*. It was mountainous, shrouded, blue-black, like a tragic precinct of the island's sunlight. The forest was called El Yunque, and it seemed to him then that those great hanging trees and all those rising mists and shadows were what was in store for him if he gave up. His life would be like that. The forest was blind. He would be lost among the high vines, trapped in their tangle, just another anonymous soul in an immensity of tall trees. The forest warned him as the sea had given him hope, but the forest's threat was worse than any he had known, of a kind of cowering adulthood, promising darkness, the scavenging of naked families. Alone, he could escape it; that forest was the fate of men who were afraid and hid. He was too young to enter it now; it was too early for him to explore such towering shadows, and to be lost now was to be lost forever.

It was after five by the time they left the beach, and they had to wait for a bus in Rio Piedras. When they got back to the old part of the city the lights were on in the plaza and there was about the whole district that atmosphere of exhaustion that follows a festival.

The milk had gone sour. Duval bought a pint from La Gloria and a ham sandwich from a street seller. Paula made a meal of them, then lay on the bed and fell asleep at once, still in her clothes. Duval covered her with a sheet and turned off the lamp. He never felt anything but tenderness for her when he saw her asleep, and he thought if he moved her even slightly she would break.

By the window, in the light from the Colorama Toy Store, he wrote what he had seen that day: the canefields, the green sea, the coconut, the lizards feeding on the rat, and the vast gloomy rain forest. The writing made him hungry; he went downstairs. But in La Gloria he reached for his money and remembered he hadn't gone to the bank. He looked for Antonio — he could have that drink he had promised and borrow some money for a *frijole*. Antonio wasn't there, and seeing all the noisy people in the bar Duval pitied himself.

He considered going for a walk: more hunger, and the sight of the rich eating in the windows of the expensive restaurants further up the Calle de San Francisco. The thought of walking bothered him for another reason: if you had no money you stayed put. He was angry — with himself, with Paula; his anger turned to fear, and the green island became again in those seconds of reproach a dangerous alien place of destitution and ruin, an intolerable trap.

In the room he looked at the pages he had written. He read a sentence: it was foolish, about the beach, an expression of pleasure. He tore out the page and crumpled it and he was about to throw it into the wastebasket when he saw the cheese.

He unwrapped it, glancing furtively at Paula. A few ants still clung to it. It was softened by the heat, and it had sweated, but it did not smell rancid. He knelt on the floor, in the darkness, and nibbled it until it was gone.

3

TAME SPIDERS DANCING on violin strings; a whiff of ice in the air; rest — wakefulness bleeding from his fingers. The images came to him at the concert; he wrote them down and admired his work. His writing calmed him like music; the concerts helped him think.

They were held every Sunday afternoon at the cultural center, a pretty house surrounded by palms on the Avenida Rivera. The people in the audience were unlikely islanders, pale Spaniards, studious blacks in neat suits, and old frail women in summer dresses. The chamber music was a soothing voiceless encouragement to thought, and the room where the concerts were given was clean and air-conditioned. Paula and Duval sat contentedly in the soft chairs breathing Mozart and cool air. It became one of their activities, like the evening walk to the cathedral or the stroll to the fort to watch the sun drop into the ocean. It was free.

In the confidential way they spoke about themselves they began hesitantly to discuss money and to worry. They had spent about a hundred dollars in a month, but even at this frugal rate — there were no more economies they could make — they knew they would have nothing left in two months. The Sunday concert was free; it cost nothing to walk — but there was food to buy, rent to pay. They said nothing about their return tickets. The knowledge of this little money was a slow ache, a dull physical pain like a smudge of guilt, and the passing days only made it keener.

"I'll have to get a job," said Duval.

"I wish I could help." Paula was bigger now; she shifted her stomach each time she moved, and she tired easily. But still she spoke of wanting to go to Rio Piedras and study Spanish. She had inquired. The course cost twenty-five dollars. They both knew it was out of the question. Her Spanish, his writing: they had come to seem like broken promises. Whatever he wrote looked incomplete, and though they contained striking islands of green imagery, they were fragments, they were linked to nothing.

Paula said, "You could go to the Hilton."

Duval resisted. The Hilton, a mile away, reminded him of what he hated and feared, everything he had left behind; humiliation.

He said he would look for a job, and thereafter, in the mornings, he put on his tie and his limp green suit and set off. Paula wished him luck and seeing her at the head of the stairs he felt sorry for her and pity for himself; he was too young for this — another future was his, not a repetition of this. As soon as he walked into the plaza he lost his will to look. He was hot, he felt tired even before he boarded the city bus. He had no practical skills, he could not speak Spanish. But worse, in the course of those days looking for a job he realized he was spending far more than if he had stayed home: bus fares, lunch, *piraguas*, newspapers. He bought the *Island Times*, the English language weekly, and looked through the classified ads. Secretary, draftsman, chemist, clerk, accountant: there was no job he could do.

But he could write. More and more in this unusual place he felt the knowledge growing in him of an impulse to write, of linking the fragments he had already set down. He could write the sad story he had already begun to live. It was the effect of the green island: surviving here proved his imagination was nimble. To choose solitude again was to become a writer, a heartless choice, rejecting a child to claim freedom.

Without telling Paula he made notes on the concert at the cultural center the next Sunday, and that night he wrote two pages about it. He described the musicians, the palms at the window, the items on the program — he compared it to a menu for a great meal. Rereading it he saw that it was stiffly enthusiastic, full of compliments and meaningless hyperbole, uncritical; yet it was printable. He had worked hard on it. He wondered if he had worked too hard. The light had been bad in the room. He had waited for Paula to sleep before he dared to begin, and twice there were sounds from Antonio's room which stopped him.

In the morning, saying that he was going to look for a job, he went to the offices of the *Island Times* and asked to see the editor. The man had his long legs on his desk, his big feet on the blotter. He had a thick black mustache and only nodded when Duval explained what he had written. He passed the pages to the man. Keeping his feet up the man read the article. Duval saw in this posture a lack of interest; he watched for a reaction and he thought he saw the man smile.

Duval said, "Can you use it?"

The man said — and Duval realized when he spoke that they were the man's first words — "We'll see."

Then Duval was embarrassed; he felt defeated and wanted to leave. In the street again he remembered that he had not mentioned money.

That Thursday he bought the *Island Times*. His piece was not in it. The news was of the filming of *Lord of the Flies* on Vieques Island, a few miles offshore. There was no mention of the concert.

He went to the Hilton. But it was not as he had imagined it, American and intimidating. The stucco was discolored by the sea air, touched by pale florets of decay; and the Puerto Rican smells of sickly fruit and *frijoles* had penetrated to the lobby. The desk clerk directed him to the personnel office, where in a waiting room there were about ten Puerto Ricans, young men and middle-aged women, who looked as if they had been there all morning. A woman at a table was speaking in Spanish to a nervous man with tough Indian features.

Duval took a seat and waited to be called forward.

"Did you see the ad too?" The man next to him was grinning. He wore a baggy linen suit and a string tie. In his southern accent was the lisp of a Spanish speaker. He had a bald wrinkled head and could have been seventy.

Duval said, "No."

"I knew you was a gringo," said the man. His mustache moved when he grinned. "The ad for their new restaurant — you ain't seen it? They looking for hands."

"What sort?"

"All kinds — in the kitchen, waiters, pearl divers, people up front to say, 'Your table is all ready, señor.' All kinds. But not the doorman. That job's as good as filled. By me."

"So they haven't hired you yet."

"No. But they sure will when they sets eyes on me." The old man tapped Duval on the shoulder and cackled. "I'se a *technician* doorman."

The woman at the desk gave Duval an application. He filled it out and in doing so invented a new man, one who was twenty-three, who had worked in several restaurants and lived in San Juan for nearly a year; married.

"Help me with this, will you, old chappie?" said the man in a whisper. "This here writing's too damned small for my eyes."

The old man — his name was Ramón Kelly — was illiterate. Duval read the application and Kelly told him what to write: born in Louisiana in 1903, a graduate of Shreveport High School; previous jobs on ships, the *Queen Mary*, the *Huey Long*, the *Andrea Doria*; married, three children. Kelly anticipated the questions, but Duval could see that Kelly was lying too, inventing a man on the job application.

"Where do I put my John Henry?"

Duval showed him.

Kelly licked the tip of the ballpoint, then touched the line and made several loops that looked convincingly like a signature. But the name was not Kelly.

The woman at the desk read Duval's application and gave him a slip of paper. She said, "Go to the restaurant — outside the building and turn left. Report to Mister Boder."

Duval did as he was told, and when he entered the restaurant, with its empty tables and smells of floor wax and fresh varnish and workmen carrying potted palms, he heard a voice say, "We got a live one." Then the man appeared and said loudly, "I hope to God you speak English!"

Over coffee, Mr. Boder said that the restaurant, which was to open in two days, was called The Beachcomber. It was part of a chain of American restaurants specializing in Polynesian food. Mr. Boder was general manager of the Los Angeles Beachcomber and had been sent to San Juan to hire waiters and supervise the opening. He was a bluff perspiring man of about fifty with capped teeth which, although perfectly shaped, were yellow from the cigars he chewed. He was friendly, he called Duval "a fellow sufferer," stuck like himself on this island of unreliable people.

Duval said, "It's a dictatorship."

"I'm glad you told me that." Mr. Boder removed his cigar from his mouth and spat into a wastebasket.

"That's what people say."

"I don't speak Spanish." He said that for a few days he had gone to bed with a copy of *L'Imparcial* and a Spanish-English dictionary, but he had abandoned the effort. He hated the island. He was newly married and missed his wife. "My second wife," he said. "She's about your age, and she's starting to whine. You married?"

"Yes."

"So I don't have to tell you," said Mr. Boder. "Ever work in a restaurant?"

Duval said he had.

Mr. Boder seemed disappointed. He said, "I hate the food business. The hours, the complaints. The kitchen's always a madhouse. It's ruined my health." He coughed disgustedly, then said, "Of all the rackets you can get in, the food business is the worst."

A Chinese-looking man came out of the kitchen. He was fat-faced and his black suit matched his scowl. He said, "There's another one in the kitchen. Show them around."

When he had gone, Duval said, "Is he Polynesian?"

"Chinese," said Mr. Boder. "It's all Chinese here. Sure, the decor is Polynesian" — he indicated an outrigger canoe which was suspended from the ceiling of woven grass — "but the food's Chinese and all the cooks are slants. That was Jimmy Lee. Did he look worried to you?"

"No," said Duval.

"He's worried. The Beachcomber himself is coming tomorrow. He's always around for the openings."

A young man came out of the kitchen. He was neatly dressed and looked like the sort of person Duval had seen at the cultural center. He said hello to Mr. Boder.

"Speak English?" said Mr. Boder.

"Yes."

"Just asking. You never know with Puerto Ricans."

"I am Cuban."

"Okay, Castro," said Mr. Boder. "That makes two. You're going to be up front with me, boys. Come over here."

Mr. Boder led them through the restaurant to the bar, which was designed to look like a bamboo and wickerwork hut in the South Seas. He said, "I'm going to tell you one or two things and I want you to remember them, because the Beachcomber's very particular. First, we don't let anyone in here that we wouldn't have in our own homes — company policy. No single broads, no hookers, and no drunks. Never recognize anyone, even if you know his name. Why? Because the woman he's with might not be his wife and maybe he told her his name's Smith. You say, 'Evening, Mister Jones,' and he's screwed. Better not to use any names at all — that's how you get tips. A little discretion. If the joint's full, steer them over here into the bar, and if you have to buy them a drink to keep them there, buy it, but don't have one yourself. Correction — you can have a Coke."

The Cuban said, "Do we have to share our tips with the waiters?"

"That's up to you," said Mr. Boder. "Now, in front of you are thirty-five, maybe forty, tropical drinks. Shark's Tooth, Jungle Juice, Pago-Pago. Forget the names. If anyone asks you what's in it just say it has rum, fruit juice, and some bitters. Confidentially, they all have the same shit in them, but you don't have to tell the Beachcomber that. You know anything about the food business, Castro?"

"Yes," he said sternly.

"Ever work up front?"

"I worked at the Hilton in Havana."

"I'm supposed to keel over," said Mr. Boder to Duval. He stared at the Cuban. "Know how important the telephone is?"

The Cuban nodded.

Mr. Boder said to Duval, "Pick up that phone and say, 'Good evening, the Beachcomber.' "

Duval lifted the phone. "Good evening, the Beachcomber."

"Say it as if you mean it."

"Good evening, the Beachcomber."

"You sound like a mortician," said Mr. Boder. "Watch me. I'll show you how it's done." He bared his yellow teeth and spoke genially into the phone.

Later that afternoon Mr. Boder said, "You're on duty tomorrow at four o'clock. Press party, so sharpen up. Don't wear that tie. You're meeting the Beachcomber himself."

Duval heard a low whistle as he left the restaurant. He turned and saw a man in a military cap with a braided visor, and more braids and buttons on a green frock coat. The trousers had a yellow stripe and white piping on the seam. It was Kelly. He said, "One cigarette before you go."

Duval shook out a cigarette and handed it over.

"I told you I'd get the job," said Kelly. Then he frowned at the cigarette. "Look at that, old chappie," he said, pinching the filter tip. "Should be tobacco there, but there's only cotton. They think they're smart and we get it! I'm going to tell the queen about that."

Duval lit the cigarette for him and said, "So you're the doorman."

Kelly smiled. "I'se a *technician* doorman. Ain't nothing I don't know about opening doors."

*　　*　　*

The Beachcomber was a potbellied man with a bullying voice and a wooden leg. At the press party he banged his cane on the carved figures and chair legs as he limped from room to room. His white hair was cut very short, his forearms stained with tattoos, and when he saw Duval he said, "Don't stand there like a goddamned Prussian. Look alive!"

He left the island the next day for a tour of the Caribbean, and then the restaurant got its first customers. There were not many; it was not the season. One of the dining rooms, The Tortuga, remained closed.

At the end of that week Duval brought his pay home. With tips it came to forty-five dollars. Paula enrolled for the Spanish class and they had their first meal in a restaurant, *arroz con pollo* at La Gloria. Duval had wanted to take her to The Beachcomber, but employees were forbidden to eat there; in any case, he doubted whether he could afford it.

The job gave him a routine. He was free for most of the day. If Paula did not have a Spanish class they walked or went to the beach — the narrow, rocky one across from the Carnegie Library. At three, Duval had a shower and then took the bus along the seafront to work. After two weeks of this he felt like a legitimate resident of the island and thought no more of leaving. Now the island which had once seemed to rock in the ocean like a raft looked vast and green. He was aware that he had spent the entire time at its edge, on the shore; the interior he imagined wild, small towns in dusty jungle where people lived ensnared. But he was safe. He had his work.

The work itself was simple. He answered the telephone and took reservations. He met customers at the door and showed them to their tables. He adjusted the volume of the Hawaiian music on the loudspeakers and kept the lights dim. The customers were mainly middle-aged couples on vacation who had come to the island because the summer prices were so low. There were young wary couples who, tanned and uneasy, he took to be honeymooners. There were secretaries, groups of three or four, who lingered over their meals and held conversations with the waiters. Now and then Duval would see a man eating alone, reading a book, and he would want to sit down and talk to the man. But he kept his place. It appalled him to think that he had in such a short time become so old, so obedient.

"The days of the free lunch are over," said Ramón Kelly, one day. "They haven't paid me for three weeks. I'm going to have to give up this nice old job."

"Do you get tips?"

"Chickenfeed," said Kelly. "My second wife lives up in Key West. She's rolling in it. I'm going up there pretty soon, open a Melanesian restaurant. Gonna get two tall Cubans for the door — black ones, these big fellas. And serve Melanesian food." He grinned.

Duval looked at Kelly's feet.

"Them's my Hoover shoes," said the old man.

Mr. Boder told him not to talk to Kelly on duty. Mr. Boder had become irritable. "You're having yourself a holiday," he said to Duval one evening when he found him reading at the telephone stand. But Mr. Boder was servile with customers and Duval noticed that his moments of servility only made him more bad-tempered with the staff, particularly the Cuban, whom he called Castro.

The Cuban resented the name and refused to say what his real name was. "I don't care," he said. "Batista was the one I hated."

"What was the Havana Hilton like?" asked Duval.

"Very nice." The Cuban clicked his tongue. "*Muchachas*."

"Whenever I hear about Havana I think of Hemingway."

"He used to come in now and then. We kept a certain wine for him — a rosé, nothing special. He always got drunk and shouted. He threw food around the table. 'Pass the bread.' He throw the bread. 'Pass the salt.' He throw the salt. Hemingway. People say he is a great writer. But they don't know. I have seen him with these eyes. He is a pig."

"Have you read his books?"

"I would never read the books of such a pig."

One meal was included. The employees ate in shifts before opening time, but not in the restaurant. They ate rice and beans in the hotel cafeteria, and Duval's half-hour always coincided with Kelly's. Kelly seemed to grow crazier. He said he was British and threatened to go back to England. "Back to Piccadilly, old chappie," he said. He complained that he still had not been paid and he said he wanted to kill Mr. Boder with a broken bottle. One evening, in the cafeteria, he asked Duval to write a letter for him. Duval said he would.

Kelly instantly pulled a crumpled sheet of paper from the pocket of his green frock coat. He said, "Got a pen?"

Duval took out his pen and smoothed the paper. He said, "Hurry up. I have to go back in a few minutes."

"I knew you'd help me," said Kelly. "Will you write what I say?"

"Of course."

"Ready?" Kelly folded his arms. "Dear President Kennedy — "

"Wait a minute," said Duval.

"Dear President Kennedy," said Kelly in his lisping drawl. "I'm an old man and I'm stuck on this goddamned island of Puerto Rico living with a widow lady. The bastards haven't paid me — you're not writing!"

"I am."

"Show me."

Duval pushed the paper to him, but Kelly lost interest in it as soon as he saw the scribble. Before Duval could begin again, Kelly said, "My old woman run out on me and the widow lady took pity. That was before the Florida business which I aim to tell you about. Bitch said she was going to Santurce and that's the last I hear from her. I couldn't find a ship. I been working on ships since I was so high and I had a right terrible life — goddamned tax people chasing me, I didn't know which way to turn. Mister President, sir, you can help me if you read this here letter — "

Duval had stopped writing. Kelly had begun to cry. In the cafeteria, in his bandsman's uniform, surrounded by chattering Puerto Ricans, the old man sat shaking his bald head. He continued to weep. The tears ran into his mustache.

But later that night Duval saw him out front. He was shutting the door of a limousine and saluting to the man who had just stepped inside.

"Boder says you're married," he said when the car drew away. "Young fella like you. Must be something wrong with you upstairs."

After that he avoided Kelly, and the days rolled past without moving him.

In the cafeteria one evening a girl sat next to him. She had the cute monkey-faced look of the prettiest Puerto Ricans — dark eyes and thick hair and a small agile body. She was a room-girl, she said, and she laughed shyly as she told him how the men were always trying to flirt with her, saying "Come in" in the morning and rushing at her in their pajamas.

Duval told her about himself, scarcely believing what he

said. "I work in The Beachcomber. I live on the Calle de San
Francisco. My wife is going to have a baby." The room-girl
was convinced; he was not. This man he was describing, this
older employee with the wife: it wasn't him.

The feeling came again, that he was living someone else's
life. He was using another man's voice, doing that man's work.
And he was surprised by how ordinary the man was, how un-
ambitious: a husband, an employee, and soon to be a father.
He listened to himself with curiosity. *I live . . . I work . . . My
wife.* The life seemed unshakably simple. How easily the
green island had abstracted him and made him this new man.

He continued to work. He could not think what else to do.
He had tried to write and had failed. He knew why. Could
anything be written in such a cramped room, in such poor
light? He fitted his life to the job: the afternoon bus, the
phone calls, the chance encounters in the cafeteria, the customers whom he hated and envied, the unvarying drone of the
Hawaiian music, the sizzle-splash of frying in the kitchen.
Without choosing he had become a different man, and he
sometimes wondered whose life he was leading, what name
he had.

The money was enough to live on, not enough to free him.
So the salary trapped him more completely than the fear of
poverty had. The job became central, the only important
thing; and his ambitions became local: to take a *público* rather
than a bus, to eat in a good restaurant rather than La Gloria,
to drink rum instead of beer.

Being away from the room for part of every day abstracted
him further, and he always returned on the late bus to find
Paula asleep, the Spanish textbook beside her, the light on.
Nearly two months had passed since they had come to the
island and she was now quite large, with new curves, the full
cones of her breasts sloping against her rising belly, the veins
showing in her tightened skin. She slept on her side; she
walked slowly; she never swam.

She studied Spanish; she didn't learn it. At La Gloria one lunchtime she began timidly to speak. She did so with difficulty, and Duval found himself interrupting, saying a sentence he had not prepared, using words he was unaware he knew and only half understood, "*Lo siento. Yo quiero el mismo, por favor.*" The stresses and accents were Puerto Rican, *Joe* for *Yo, meemo* for *mismo*.

* * *

Whose voice was that?

"Jake!"

He was in bed, being shaken by a damp hand. Paula faced him with tangled hair and her look of worry intensified by the wrinkles of sleep that creased the side of her face.

"Wake up — I'm scared." There was a low roar at the window: the sea, the fury of a distant bus, the wind — he couldn't say.

"What's wrong?"

"I dreamed I had the baby," she sobbed. "It was terrible. You weren't there — oh, God, it hurt. Then they held him up for me to see. Jake, his face was all mangled. It was covered with blood."

Too soon, he thought. This worry shouldn't be mine. But he tried to accept it. He said, "All babies look like that — you've seen pictures of them."

"No — it wasn't the blood," she said, and she grew very quiet, whispering her fearfulness. "It was all deformed. The baby's face was twisted and it was crying. 'It's yours,' they said, 'it's yours.' It was horrible."

He didn't know what to say. But he knew her fear. He saw the infant's bloody distorted face, twisted in accusation. He held Paula and then he was asleep.

In the morning he struggled to wake. The summer heat, the dampness in the air lay motionless against him; pressure, keeping him down. He didn't hear the voices from the street, only the song "*El Pescador*," with its refrain, *corazón, corazón;* its harsh Puerto Rican sadness. He no longer heard the sea. The sea was drowned by the wind; lost. He had ceased to see the island, its greenness. He had withdrawn to his own island, the room, the woman, the job.

4

PAULA DID NOT tell him how the Spanish classes reminded her of her old life, the pleasure of uninterrupted study in a clean room, the security of a narrow bed. It was the life she had led before she had met Duval: her girlhood. She wanted it back. She had come to hate the changeless green of the island, the late-summer tinge of yellow exhaustion in the color. She did not tell him how, when he was at work, she never left the room; how she would sleep and wake and think it was another day, and sleep and wake again and imagine that in the space of a few hours she had endured days of seclusion. She had said nothing about the doctor she had seen. The office was dusty, the doctor sweating into his shirt, not noticing his smeared instruments. He smiled (the usual reaction: kindly people tried to share her joy) and after examining her said, "You are — what? — about five months." She was nearly eight. She took all her questions back to the room unasked.

One hot night she told Duval, "We can give it away."

"What do you mean?" But he was stalling; he knew.

She explained that she had written to a friend in Boston, an old roommate, and the girl had supplied the names of three adoption agencies. Heartbreaking names: one was "The Home for Little Wanderers."

Duval said, "They put them in orphanages."

"No," she said. "They give them to people who can't have children themselves. They're very fussy, too — they check up on the people. They sort of inspect them."

"Then they just hand the kid over."

"Don't pretend to be shocked! You don't want the baby!" She was shouting. In a moment she would cry.

He said, "Do you?"

"I don't want to live like this."

"This is how it would be."

"It could be different," she said. "You could finish college, get your degree — "

"It would always be like this — a room, a job." He could see she was frightened. "We'd quarrel."

"I don't want to fight with you."

He said, "Married people fight."

"Single people fight, too."

"They can walk away."

She said, "That's what you want to do with me — you want to walk away and pretend I don't exist. Admit it! You want to leave me."

"What do you want me to do?"

"I don't know," she said. She had come to dislike her body; she did not recognize it as her own, it was so swollen and unreliable. And she feared the arrival of the baby — feared it most because she knew she would love it and want to keep it, and her life would be over, like that. "Help me," she said. "I feel so ugly."

He said, "You know that doorman, Kelly — the old guy I told you about? I asked him about his job once, and he started to talk about some joint he worked at in Florida. He's got this funny way of talking. He said, 'They wanted me inside once. I was young like you. I said, no sir — I like it out here. Fresh air, meet new people. That's why I'm still here,' he said, 'but I ain't young no more and I don't like it.' "

Paula said, "You're going to leave me."

"I was talking about Kelly."

"We have to decide." She lay on the bed and clasped her stomach as if tenderly enfolding the child. She said, "The poor thing," and then, "No — I don't care what you do, I won't give him away!"

She was insisting he choose, but it seemed to him as if he were past any choice and his life would continue like this, summer after summer, the heat deadening him to the days.

He went to the toilet, which was in darkness. He felt for the light cord and pulled it. For seconds there was stillness, and then the floor moved with cockroaches the heat had enlivened. They ran like large glossy drops and were gone. He had only to wait to see it solved.

The next day was Sunday. Paula awoke, and as if the sleep had been no more than a pause in their conversation she said in an alert accusing voice, "Make up your mind — what are you going to do?"

"We still have a few months."

"Six weeks," she said sharply. "What is it you want?"

He couldn't say, *I want to be a writer.* It seemed as ridiculous as, *I want to be president.* It was partly superstition: saying it might make it untrue. And yet he saw his books, a shelf of them, as clearly as if he had already written them. The conviction had stuck — not that he was to become a writer, but that he had been one secretly for as long as he could remember. To reveal the ambition was to spoil it. And more, to say it was to commit himself to proving it. He wanted someone to verify it in him, to read his face and say, *You are a writer.*

He said, "Do you want to marry me?"

"If we got married we'd be divorced in two years."

He turned away. "Maybe we've had our marriage."

"Is it over so soon? Is that all?" She became angry. "I want more than this."

"So do I!"

"I hate you for hesitating — "

"Hesitating?"

"For bringing me here," she said. "I don't think I could forgive you, even if you did marry me."

He said, "I wish I was forty years old and my life was behind me."

"That shows how young you are," she said, almost exulting. "Men of forty aren't old! You don't know anything."

Later, walking down the Calle de San Francisco to lunch at La Gloria, she said, "In six weeks there are going to be three of us. Think about that and you won't feel so smart."

But having said it she grew sad and couldn't eat, and after lunch she said it was too hot for the beach.

Duval went back to the room with her and dressed for work. It was only two o'clock; he was not due at the restaurant until five. He left her on the bed with her Spanish book, in the posture that put her to sleep. A bus in the plaza bore the destination sign LOIZA. He boarded the bus and rode to the end of the line.

Loiza was not as he had imagined, a shady corner at the forest's edge, a frontier. It was simply a leaning signpost where the bus stopped and turned around. The street, wide and useless, continued through a drab suburb of stucco bungalows. There were some palms along the roadside, but they were not green, and dead fronds like the ruined plumage of an enormous bird lay in the broken street. Political slogans with their enclosing exclamation marks were painted on the bungalow walls and on some lampposts were pictures of the president, Muñoz Marin. No sun, only a low cloud as gray as metal radiated humid heat. Duval walked down the sidewalk and saw more of the Sunday emptiness, cracked bungalows, grass growing through blisters in the asphalt, and from behind the dusty hedges the radio's tin rhumba, "*El Pescador*" and *corazón*.

He walked to a road junction and ahead saw a parking lot filled with cars, and above a sign, CANTO GALLO. He welcomed the noise and hurried toward it.

It was a *galleria*, a cockpit. He bought a ticket for the middle tier, but as he started through the door he faced confusion

— men counting money, men running down the passage, gamblers quarreling — and to avoid them he slipped through a side door and down a short flight of stairs.

The room smelled of straw and chicken droppings and was stacked with wooden cages holding small skinny roosters. They scratched and squawked, but there was in their crowing something still of the farmyard, the shady unfenced Puerto Rican plot with its standpipe and sprinklings of corn. They fussed, yet looked calm, and Duval found it odd to see them in these vertical piles, crammed in such a small space.

He wandered around the room, looking closely at the birds, noticing their bright eyes, the shine of their feathers, the wrinkled bunch of scrotumlike tissue draped on their heads, their oversized feet and stained claws. He heard Paula speaking, saw her face, and in her face a demand. *Choose, choose*, she was saying.

But each time he framed a reply, a shout went up from behind the wall of this fowlcoop, in the cockpit — triumphant cries of yelling laughter. The cries became more frequent and lost the laughter, and they were accompanied by a stamping of many feet which shook the beams over his head. The howling sounded neither Spanish nor English; it was no language; it was encouragement, anger, jeering, the noise of people watching a small hero, an insignificant victim; a mob's praise.

The crouching roosters on their shelves of cages seemed to hear it. They stuck their heads through the wooden bars and jerked their necks, so their jeweled staring eyes turned in wonderment. Duval paced the room. The cocks pecked hard at their padlocks. *It's up to you*, she was saying.

He was about to go away — to leave the *gallería* entirely — when three men entered the small room. They were excited, jabbering in Spanish, arguing without facing each other. One stayed at the door glowering at Duval. The other two went to the stack of cages and took out two cocks, a black one, a brown one, and quickly trussed them with lengths of cord.

The birds fought and flapped while their legs were tied, then lay still, two parcels of feathers, like a pair of brushes. The men were attaching spurs to the birds' legs when the man at the door spoke.

"Go," he said crossly to Duval and gestured for him to leave.

Duval went upstairs and took a seat in the middle tier. Most of the seats were empty, but near him, in the section that surrounded the circle of the pit, the seats were full, and it was only there, up front, that he saw women, two or three. It was like the interior of a primitive circus. The roof seemed propped on shafts of dusty sunlight; and the rough unpainted wood and the dust rising from the shallow pit and its suffocating smallness lent it an unmistakable air of cruelty.

Brass scales were brought out, the chains and pans jangling, and the trussed cocks were placed in the pans and balanced. The two pairs of bound feet hovered at the same level. The scales were raised for the audience to see. There was chattering throughout the ritual of weighing, but as the scales were removed the gallery became frenzied — men called across the pit, shouting numbers and waving dollar bills. One man vaulted the low fence and hurried across the pit to shake a wad of money in another's frowning face.

The birds were untied, but instead of releasing them the owners faced each other, holding them forward and slowly circling, keeping the beaks a few inches apart, struggling against the flapping wings and angry reaching beaks. The cocks' eyes were blazing as the men solemnly set them down.

Now Duval saw the spurs, inch-long claws clamped to their legs, which gave them a fierce strutting look. The black one began to run around the margin of the pit.

The squawks were drowned by the shouts from the audience, and the birds flew at each other. They did not appear to use the spurs. They fluttered a foot from the ground, seeming to balance on their downthrust wings, and they threw their heads forward and bore down, snatching and pecking with their beaks. The brown one rose higher, pecked harder and pinioned the black one clumsily with clawing feet. He beat him down with his wings and drove his beak into the black one's head. They tumbled in the dust, crazily magnetized, and then chased each other in circles around the pit, with outstretched necks, moving gracefully flatfooted, driving dust and feathers into the air.

No, thought Duval, and he was deafened by the cries from the audience. The brown cock flew and settled against the black one, plucking the reddened head.

The black one had started to weaken. One wing was askew, and it scraped the ground with it and tottered on it as it toiled away from the other. The brown one screamed and beat its wings and attacked again. The wing flaps, the flutter of feathers simulating the opening of a Chinese fan, sounded harmless, but it masked the damage. When they were close Duval could see how the cocks' heads were both swollen and their feathers ragged. The audience was excited, beginning to stamp the supporting planks of the gallery and shake the wooden benches.

Like old hindering skirts, the wings of the black cock hung down, and he wobbled in panic around the pit, the brown one behind him, leaping and pecking. The black one fell and crooked his feet against the brown one's attack, and finally, in a helpless effort to fight back, offered his bleeding head to the other's furious beak.

There were cheers; the owners stepped in; the cheering stopped. The audience showed no further interest in the birds. Money was changing hands and men had gathered in groups to argue about the result.

Duval followed the owners back to the fowlcoop. The cocks were placed on a table and examined. The brown one which had been so lively was feebly twitching its legs as its owner ran his fingers through the tufts of feathers to search for wounds. The black one lay as if dead; the scrotal comb was torn and its head was split all over and leaking blood. The owner prodded it gently and murmured in Spanish. Then he lifted its damaged eyelids and said sadly, "*Mira*." He showed the empty eye sockets of the blinded bird.

No, thought Duval again, and back in the street, walking to the bus stop through the suburb that now had a look of pure horror, his reflection came to him whole: *I will never get married*.

5

THE SUN, glimmering and enlarged by cloud, was at the level of the treetops, balanced on the upper thickness of palm fronds, as Duval walked to work. The opposite side of the street was marked by the sunset's pickets of shadow, flung from the palm trunks, and in this broken light women strolled, some singly, some in pairs.

Mr. Boder was in front of the restaurant talking to Kelly. What struck Duval at once was that Mr. Boder was crowding the old man as he spoke and peering into his face, almost bumping him with his nose. When Duval spoke Mr. Boder stepped back.

"Looking at the action," said Mr. Boder, with the kind of disguising heartiness he used on customers. He nodded at the women.

Kelly looked crestfallen. He said nothing.

"Professionals," said Duval. He winked at Kelly. "*Por la noche*."

"I'd like to jump all over that one," said Mr. Boder. He licked his lips. "I'm overdue for a strange piece."

It was a vicious phrase. Duval saw him taste it. The women wore tight dresses with a slash to show their legs, and they walked with a slow rolling movement and swung large handbags. But it was the shoes that gave them away. The spike heels were worn down from their continual pacing, giving them an unsteadiness that made them lurch tipsily every few steps.

Duval said, "That one's smiling. I think she likes you."

Mr. Boder's face tightened, as if he had been mocked. He said, "Come inside. I want to know why you're late." And without another word he entered the restaurant.

Kelly said, "Oh, me."

"What's wrong?"

"I just got me walking papers."

"He fired you?" Duval was puzzled. "What for?"

"They owes me money. I axed him for it. He told me I was sassing him." But Kelly was smiling. "I'se a doorman without no door."

"You're joking."

"Boy," said Kelly. "You better go on in there or you're going to be out on your ear, too."

Duval went inside and put on his Beachcomber blazer. In the foyer of the restaurant he saw Mr. Boder seated at the telephone.

Mr. Boder said, "I've been doing your work for you. Look at these reservations." He showed Duval the diary with the column of names in his oversize handwriting. "Now, where the hell have you been?"

"Waiting for a bus." He would not say he had been to a cockfight. The sight had terrified him and he could not repeat what he had seen: the bright jeweled eye plucked out, the scrap of white tissue in the eye socket, the dripping blinded head of the bird.

"If you're late again I'll dock your salary — your wife won't like that, will she?" Mr. Boder stood up. "What did that crazy old man tell you out front?"

Duval said angrily, "Did you fire him?"

Mr. Boder did not reply immediately. He walked toward the bar and then, as if remembering, turned and said loudly, "You mind your own business, sonny, if you know what's good for you."

Duval picked up the diary. It was the Cuban's night off;

Sundays were quiet. A dozen customers came and went, and the waiters were impatient, drumming their fingers on their trays, complaining in murmurs, and watching for the front door to open.

Duval went outside. Kelly was gone.

The next night there was a Puerto Rican at the door. It was only when Duval saw the baggy wrinkled uniform on the man that he realized how tall Kelly had been. Duval avoided speaking to Mr. Boder that night, and at closing time, he was indignant and sad. He wanted a drink. It was a hotel rule that employees off duty were to leave the premises. The casino, the coffee shop, the pool, the bars were closed to him; and he knew he could be fired for breaking that rule.

Duval went to the hotel's veranda bar, where the drinks were slightly cheaper than inside, and sat and had three shots of rum. He drank them straight, in the Puerto Rican way, finishing with a glass of water. Then he stumbled down the gravel driveway to the bus stop. No one had seen him.

A woman came toward him from behind a palm, her heels clicking on the sidewalk, the revealing wobble in her step. Her hair was drawn back tightly and even in the street lamp's poor light he could see that her dress was soiled. She was short and had a small mouth stamped in her sharp face.

She said, "Want a date, mister?"

"How much?"

"Ten dollars."

Duval went through his pockets. He found a dollar and some change. He had spent the rest of his tips at the bar. He said, "I'm nineteen — don't I get a discount?"

She recognized the word and laughed. "Even the young ones, they pay me."

"I don't have any money."

"*Nada por nada,*" she said. "*Buenos noches, chico.*"

"Wait," said Duval. "Where are you from — San Juan?"

"Habana."

"You like San Juan?"

"I like this." She touched her thighs and jerked her hips at him. She leered: gold teeth.

That aroused him, and though it was after midnight when he got back to the old part of the city he went to La Gloria. It was closed; a man was stacking chairs on the bar. In the plaza he could see the homeless boys sleeping curled up on the stone benches, small still corpses on the slabs. He walked up the Calle de San Francisco. The street was empty, but he kept walking, looking in doorways. He turned into a narrow cobblestone street and headed down the hill, past darkened shops and small hotels, feeling the rum's warmth still in his throat and a fatigue from work that gave him a nervous inaccurate strength and a quick stride.

He barely heard the woman's greeting. She had been seated on a bench; she rose and said hello as he passed. The sound reached him. She was asking for a cigarette.

He offered her one and lit it, and in the match flare he saw her lined face, the dress a bit too big, the firelit strand of black hair loose at her eyes. She looked cautious, almost afraid.

He said, "What's your name?"

"Anna," she said, and glanced down the street. "You want to go with me?"

"Yes," he said.

"Five dollars."

"I don't have five dollars."

"Four dollars," she said. "Let we go."

He fished in his pockets, knowing what he would bring out. He showed her the dollar, he rattled the change.

She said, "You don't respect me."

"Please," he said.

"No." She walked away. He followed her down the sidewalk, and when she stopped before a storefront he was encouraged.

"Anna," he said softly.

"You see?" She was tapping the plate glass of the shop window.

He saw a rack of shoes and looked away. They were tiny; children's shoes, small laced things with price tags, mounted on stands.

"Look," she said, urging him. "These things cost money."

It was too late; he had seen the pathetic shoes and the prices, and all his desire died.

* * *

He entered the room, but did not switch on the light. He undressed in the darkness and slipped beneath the sheet. Paula rolled toward him. She took his head and drew it to her, and he could hear the slow thump of her heart against her breast. He nestled against her, hating the thought that he had betrayed her and was, embracing and kissing her, betraying her still.

* * *

Paula awoke in tears, and he felt a helpless sorrow for her as she sobbed. The child, her stomach, shook.

"It's not fair to me," she said. "It's not fair to him. The poor baby."

He knew what to say, but not how to say it. She was so easily frightened.

She said, "We don't have much time."

Choose, she was saying. But he had chosen long ago; he had discovered his small green soul on the island, its solitary inward conceit scribbled differently from hers, and now he could read the scribble.

"Poor Kelly," he said. He saw him, the clown, the limp mustache, the green frock coat and braided cap. The old man moped toward him, chattering, blinded, indicating his flat shoes with a crooked finger: *Them's my Hoover shoes.*

Paula said, "I'm not staying here much longer — I'm not having my baby on this miserable island. I'm going to catch a plane while they'll still let me. Women can't fly if they're more than eight months pregnant." She looked at him strangely. "You didn't even know that."

"What about the tickets?"

"I've been to the bank. We've got the airfare now — enough for two tickets home."

"After that?"

"It's up to you."

" 'My baby' — that's what you said."

She cried again, hearing her own words repeated. "I don't want him," she said, her mouth curling sorrowfully. "I want to go back to school and do well. I want to marry someone who loves me. I want a nice house."

Duval thought: *I don't want any of those things;* but he wouldn't upset her by saying what he did want.

She said, "And I don't want to be a failure."

"You won't fail."

"What do you know?" she said. "What do you do after you give a child away?"

"You start again," he said. "Alone."

"You have no more chances. If you fail then, you have nothing."

"No," he said, but he only said it to oppose her, to offer encouragement.

"Nothing at all," she said bitterly. "*Nada.*"

"It's a gamble," he said.

"It's a human sacrifice."

* * *

He was deliberately late for work that day, but instead of confronting him Mr. Boder ignored him. Duval heard him shouting in the kitchen.

The Cuban was listening, too. He said, "I hate that pig."

"Then why do you put up with him?"

"This isn't my country," he said. "They could throw me out." He kicked gloomily at the carpet. "I got a wife and two *niños.*"

Mr. Boder came out of the kitchen. "What's up — nothing to do? Who's watching that phone?"

The Cuban said, "I am."

"Come here, Castro. I've got a job for you." Mr. Boder went close to Duval and peered at him. He said, "Keep it up. You're asking for it."

Duval stared at him. He had said that to Kelly.

"Move that chair. Someone's going to trip over it."

"It's not in the way."

"Are you deaf?"

Duval moved the chair, and in this tiny act of obedience he saw humiliating surrender. But his timidity was for hire: he was to blame.

"He's worried," said the Cuban later. "The vice chancellor of the university is coming from Rio Piedras with his whole family. He wants to make a good figure."

It was true. At nine-thirty the man came. He was a thin dapper man with a narrow head and a mustache fringing his upper lip. He held his young son's hand, and his wife followed, shepherding two older girls in white dresses.

But there was a further surprise. At ten the Beachcomber arrived. It was wholly unexpected and Duval could see the shock on Mr. Boder's face when the door swung open and the Beachcomber dragged his wooden leg through and tapped his way forward, rocking on the leg, balancing with the cane. The Puerto Rican waiters barely recognized him, and watched the way he moved with the contempt they offered all cripples.

"Boder!" said the Beachcomber before Mr. Boder could speak.

"This is a pleasant surprise," said Mr. Boder, regaining himself, grinning, hesitating in a bow.

"I was in Santo Domingo," said the Beachcomber. His hair was slightly longer, but he wore the same short-sleeved Hawaiian shirt that showed his tattoos.

"Fascinating place," said Mr. Boder.

"They shot Trujillo this afternoon," said the Beachcomber.

"I took the first plane and got the hell out. Why is this place so goddamned empty?"

"Slow night," said Mr. Boder. "Very unusual. Right this way."

The Beachcomber paused and shifted his weight from his good leg to the cane. He said, "Looks like Thursday at the city morgue."

Mr. Boder, smiling, did not appear to hear. He fussed with the reservations diary and then started to speak.

"Get me a drink," said the Beachcomber and moved off heavily, in the direction of the dining room.

"Right you are," said Mr. Boder, still grinning, showing his yellow capped teeth at the Beachcomber's back.

The waiters had gathered in a little group by one of the carved Polynesian statues. They were whispering. Duval heard *Trujillo* and *muerte*.

Mr. Boder brought a tall glass to where the Beachcomber was sitting. He sat sloppily, his wooden leg propped on a chair, scratching his tattoos, and squinting crossly at the nearly empty dining room. Duval saw him as a fraud, a tycoon in old clothes, a figure of crass romance. The Beachcomber was staring at the vice chancellor, who was deep in conversation with a waiter. They were talking about Trujillo. Another waiter came over to confirm it. Duval heard *verdad*. In minutes the whole restaurant knew what the Beachcomber had only muttered.

"Very unusual," Mr. Boder was saying, bowing as he spoke. Duval was behind him.

Mr. Boder turned and hissed, "Where's Castro?"

"I don't like it," the Beachcomber was saying. "You can do better than this, Boder."

"Eating," said Duval.

"Get him," said Mr. Boder. "And make it snappy. While you're at it get another cloth for the table — this one's filthy. Oh, and don't think" — Mr. Boder was still hissing, but he was also smiling, half-turned to the Beachcomber — "don't think

I didn't notice you were late for work. I've got something to say to you later. Now move."

"Boder — " Duval heard the Beachcomber say as he left the dining room.

He went through the kitchen to the hotel cafeteria. The waiters had brought the news here of Trujillo's assassination and there were groups of Puerto Ricans in the corridor talking excitedly. An elderly Negro moved among them slapping his mop on the tiles.

Duval was lost in thought. *Your wife wouldn't like that.* He tried to swallow his anger. Five minutes had passed; ten before he got to the cafeteria. He paused at the door, hating the noise, the plates banging, the voices. They were talking about Trujillo. Already the repetition of this news irritated Duval. He saw the Cuban, eating alone, forking food to his mouth.

Twenty minutes: nothing. But it was too long. In that small delay was his refusal. He winced, thinking of Mr. Boder's anger. He could never again return to the restaurant. He was finished here, as lightly as he had begun.

It was — this hesitation — as much of a choice as he needed to make. And he had hung up his blazer and was walking past the floodlit palms of the hotel driveway before he realized the enormity of what he had done. Then Mr. Boder, the Beachcomber, the waiters, everyone there seemed suddenly very small, no larger than children; and children had no memory.

It was so simple to go. Now he knew how. You walked away without a sound and kept walking. Beyond the lush hotel garden he saw light, but it was the moon behind the trees that lit them so strangely, darkening the green, like smoke beginning.

He decided to walk the mile home. As he walked on the sea road to the old part of the city the moon rose, seeming to wet the palms with its light. The wind was on the sea, and the waves tumbled like lost cargoes of silver smashing to pieces on the beach.

ACKNOWLEDGEMENTS

THANKS ARE DUE to Dr. Milton Rumbellow, Chairman of the Department of Comparative Literature, Yourgrau College (Wyola Campus), for generously allowing me first a small course load and then an indefinite leave of absence from my duties; to Mrs. Edith Rumbellow for many kindnesses, not the least of which was her interceding on my behalf; to the trustees of Yourgrau College for a grant-in-aid, to the John Simon Guggenheim Memorial Foundation for extending my fellowship to two years, and to the National Endowment for the Arts, without whose help this book could not have been written; to Miss Sally-Ann Fletcher, of Wyolatours, for ably ticketing and cross-checking a varied itinerary, and to Miss Denise Humpherson, of the British Tourist Authority, who provided me with a map of the cycling paths in the areas of England lived in by Matthew Casket; to Mrs. Mabel Nittish for arranging the sublet of my Wyola apartment and providing me a folding bike.

As with many other biographers of minor West Country dialect poets, Casket's output was so small that he could feed himself only by securing remunerative employment in unrelated fields. I am grateful for the cooperation of his former employers — in particular to Bewlence & Sons (Solid Fuels), Ltd., Western Feeds, Yeovil Rubber Goods, and Raybold &

Squarey (Drugs Division), Ltd., for allowing me access to their in-house files and providing me with hospitality over a period of weeks; and especially to Mrs. Ronald Bewlence for endlessly informative chats and helping me dispose of a bike, and Mrs. Margaret Squarey, F.P.S., for placing herself entirely at my disposal and sharing with me her wide knowledge of poisons and toxic weeds.

At a crucial stage in my ongoing research, I was privileged to meet Mrs. Daphne Casket Hebblewhite, who, at sixty-two, still remembered her father's run of bad luck. For three months of hospitality at "Limpets" and many hours of tirelessly answering my questions, I must express my thanks and, with them, my sorrow that the late Mrs. Hebblewhite was not alive to read this memorial to her father, which she and I both felt was scandalously overdue. It was Mrs. Hebblewhite who, by willing them to me, gave me access to what few Casket papers exist, and who graciously provided me with introductions to Casket's surviving relations — Miss Fiona Slaughter, Miss Gloria Wyngard, and Miss Tracy Champneys; I am happy to record here my debt for their warmth and openness to a stranger to their shores. Miss Slaughter acceded to all my requests, as well as taking on some extensive chauffering; Miss Wyngard unearthed for me a second copy of Casket's only book, but annotated in his own hand, enabling me to speculate on what he might have attempted in revised form had he had the means to do so, and allowing me the treasured memento of another warm friendship and our weeks in Swanage; Miss Champneys made herself available to me in many ways, giving me her constant attention, and it is to her efforts, as well as those of Ruck & Grutchfield, Barristers-at-Law, that I owe the speedy end of what could have been a piece of protracted litigation. To Señorita Luisa Alfardo Lizardi, who kept Mrs. Hebblewhite's house open to me after her late mistress's tragic passing and was on call twenty-four hours a day, I am more grateful than I can sufficiently express here.

Special thanks must go to the staff of Broomhill Hospital, Old Sarum, and particularly to Miss Francine Kelversedge, S.R.N., for encouraging me in my project during a needed rest from exhausting weeks of research. Colonel and Mrs. Hapgood Chalke came to my rescue at a turning point in my Broomhill sojourn; to them I owe more than I can adequately convey, and to their dear daughter, Tamsin, my keenest thanks for guiding my hand and for her resourcefulness in providing explanations when they were in short supply. To Dr. Winifred Sparrow, Director of Broomhill, I can only state my gratitude for waiving payment for my five months of convalescence; and to Stones & Sons, Tobacconists, Worsfold's Wine Merchants, and Hine's Distilleries, all of Old Sarum, my deepest thanks for understanding, prompt delivery, and good will in circumstances that would have had lesser tradesmen seeking legal redress.

I am grateful for the hospitality I received during the weeks I spent at the homes of Mr. and Mrs. Warner Ditchley, Mrs. R. B. Ollenshaw, Dr. and Mrs. F. G. Cockburn, Major and Mrs. B. P. Birdsmoor, and the late Mrs. J. R. W. Gatacre, all of Devizes, as well as for the timely intervention of Miss Helena Binchey, of Devizes, who, on short notice, placed a car at my disposal in order that I could visit the distant places Casket had known as a child. The Rev. John Punnel, of St. Alban's Primary School, Nether Wallop, provided me with safe harbor as well as a detailed record of Casket's meager education; he kindly returned Miss Binchey's car to Devizes, and it was Mrs. Dorothy Punnel who took me on a delightfully informal tour of the attic bedroom in the dorm, which cannot be very different today from what it was in 1892, when, just prior to his expulsion on an unproved charge of lewdness, Casket was a boarder.

I feel lucky in being able to record my appreciation to Pamela, Lady Grapethorpe, of Nether Wallop Manor, for admitting a footsore traveler and allowing him unlimited use of her house; for her introducing him to the Nether Wallop Flying Club and Aerodrome and to Miss Florence Fettering, who expertly piloted him to Nettlebed, in West Dorset, and accompanied him throughout his visit in the village where Casket was employed as a twister and ropeworker at the gundry. I am obliged also to Miss Vanessa Liphook, of The Bull Inn, Nettlebed, for very kindly spiriting me from Nettlebed to Compton Valence, where Casket, then a lay brother, worked as a crofter at the friary after the failure of his book. It is thanks to the good offices of Miss Liphook, and her indefatigable Riley, that I was able to tour the South Coast resorts where Casket, in his eighties and down on his luck, found seasonal employment as a scullion and kitchen hand; for their faith in my project and their sumptuous hospitality, I am indebted to the proprietors of The Frog and Nightgown, Bognor Regis; The Raven, Weymouth; The Kings Arms, Bridport; Sprackling House, Eype; and The Grand Hotel, Charmouth. To Miss Josephine Slape, of Charmouth, where Casket died of consumption, I owe the deepest of bows for the loan of a bicycle when it was desperately needed; and to the staff of the Goods Shed, Axminster, I am grateful for their speeding the bicycle back to its owner.

To Mrs. Annabel Frampton, of the British Rail ticket office, Axminster, my sincere thanks for being so generous with a temporarily embarrassed researcher; and to Dame Marina Pensel-Cripps, casually met on the 10:24 to London, but fondly remembered, I am grateful for an introduction to the late Sir Ronald and to Lady Mary Bassetlaw, of Bassetlaw Castle, at which the greater part of this book was written over an eventful period of months as tragic as they were blissful. It is impossible for me adequately to describe the many ways in which Lady Mary aided me in the preparation of this work; she met every need, overcame every obstacle, and replied to every question, the last of which replies, and by far the hardest, was her affirmative when I asked her to be my wife. So, to my dear Mary, the profoundest of thank yous: this book should have been a sonnet.

Lastly, to Miss Ramona Slupski, Miss Heidi Lim Choo Tan, Miss Piper Vathek, and Miss Joylene Aguilar Garcia Rosario, all of the Graduate Section of British Studies, Yourgrau College, my thanks for collating material and answering swiftly my transatlantic letters and demands; to Miss Gudrun Naismith, for immaculately typing many drafts of this work and deciphering my nearly illegible and at times tormented handwriting, my deepest thanks. And to all my former colleagues at Yourgrau (Wyola Campus), who, by urging me forward in my work, reversed my fortunes, my grateful thanks for assisting me in this undertaking.

MORE ABOUT PENGUINS
AND PELICANS

For further information about books available from Penguins please write to Dept EP, Penguin Books Ltd, Harmondsworth, Middlesex UB7 0DA.

In the U.S.A.: For a complete list of books available from Penguins in the United States write to Dept DG, Penguin Books, 299 Murray Hill Parkway, East Rutherford, New Jersey 07073.

In Canada: For a complete list of books available from Penguins in Canada write to Penguin Books Canada Ltd, 2801 John Street, Markham, Ontario L3R 1B4.

In Australia: For a complete list of books available from Penguins in Australia write to the Marketing Department, Penguin Books Australia Ltd, P.O. Box 257, Ringwood, Victoria 3134.

In New Zealand: For a complete list of books available from Penguins in New Zealand write to the Marketing Department, Penguin Books (N.Z.) Ltd, P.O. Box 4019, Auckland 10.

In India: For a complete list of books available from Penguins in India write to Penguin Overseas Ltd, 706 Eros Apartments, 56 Nehru Place, New Delhi 110019.